THE DAMNED DON'T DIE

The Reed Ferguson Mystery Series, Book 16

RENÉE PAWLISH

D1532431

The Damned Don't Die
A Reed Ferguson Mystery

First Digital Edition published by Creative Cat Press
copyright 2017 by Renée Pawlish

ACKNOWLEDGMENTS

The author gratefully acknowledges all those who helped in the writing of this book, especially: Beth Treat and Janice Horne. If I've forgotten anyone, please accept my apologies.

To all my beta readers: I am in your debt!
Maureen Anderson, Bill Baker, Suzanne S. Barnhill, Renee Boomershine, Van Brollini, Kate Dionne, Irene David, Betty Jo English, Tracy Gestewitz, Patti Gross, Barbara Hackel, Eileen Hill, Elisabeth Huhn, JoAnn Ice, Joyce Kahaly, David King, Ray Kline, Maxine Lauer, Lyric McKnight, Debbie McNally, Karen Melde, Judi Moore, Becky Neilsen, Gerry Nelson, Ronnie Nelson, Ann Owen, Janice Paysinger, Charlene Pruett, Fritzi Redgrave, David Richard, Chance Rideout, Judith Rogow, Becky Serna, Tracie Ann Setliff, Bev Smith, Al Stevens, Latonya Stewart, Ted Stewart, Joyce Stumpff, Morris Sweet, Patricia Thursby, Georgi Tileston, Jo Trowbridge, Marlene van Matre, Shelly Voss, Lu Wilmot, Mike Wynn

CHAPTER ONE

"Reed Ferguson, don't you look at me like I murdered some-one." Shirley Durocher was walking down the sidewalk in front of my condo building, which is in the Uptown neighborhood, just north of downtown Denver. "I know you're a detective, but that doesn't mean that everyone is up to no good."

"No, Mrs. Durocher," I said politely. I was squinting at her, but I wasn't sure that meant I was looking at her funny.

"It's Miss, and please, call me Shirley. Miss Durocher sounds so old."

Shirley Durocher – a short, spitfire of a woman – was perhaps a little older than my own mother, and I automatically showed her the same courtesy and respect that I would've shown my mother.

"It's a pleasant day, nice for October," I said, still trying for courtesy.

Shirley playfully slapped my arm, then harrumphed in the same way that my own mother did so well. But she seemed a bit flirtatious, which kind of creeped me out. Then she gazed with

1

beady dark eyes at Ace and Deuce Smith, my downstairs neighbors, who'd been talking with me before she walked up.

She pointed a bony finger at them. "You two need to watch what you're doing, too," she went on, her voice a warble and tinged with a southern twang. "You need to stay out of trouble."

"Yes, ma'am," they said in unison.

Shirley glanced around and poked her fingers through her dark hair. "I don't know what's happening in this neighborhood, things going on late at night, people spying on my house, but I tell you what, at our neighborhood meeting tonight, I'll have a say about that." Her eyes darted from Ace to Deuce. "Are you boys out gallivanting around the neighborhood, maybe snooping around my place, when you should be at home?"

"Of course not." They again spoke at the same time.

Ace shifted from foot to foot nervously, and Deuce looked everywhere but at her. With the same blond hair cropped short and snowy gray eyes, the brothers could've been twins, and right now they looked – undeservedly – like chastened little boys. I'd affectionately dubbed them the Goofball Brothers because even though the elevator may not have reached the top floor, they were smart in their own way. They were also the kindest and most loyal friends a person could ask for, and they'd become like brothers to me.

"Ace and Deuce aren't doing anything wrong," I said.

"Well, all right, then," Shirley pronounced. Then she gave me a sly smile.

Was she really flirting with me? I cleared my throat and looked away.

She fixed all three of us with a stern look, then continued on down the sidewalk. She soon passed Mr. Bonifacio's house. He was sitting on the porch, and they stared at each other as she walked by. Ace, Deuce, and I tried not to watch her, and yet all three of us did, none of us daring to move lest we incur more of her unwarranted wrath. Then she went on to her house and disappeared inside.

"She scares me," Deuce finally said, breaking the awkward silence.

Ace let out a long breath. "Me, too. She reminds me of Aunt Clarice." He looked at Deuce. "You remember her?"

Deuce nodded. "She wasn't very nice."

"No, she wasn't," Ace said.

"And what does she mean about us spying on her?" Deuce asked. "We wouldn't do that."

Ace turned to me. "You're not investigating Shirley, are you? I mean, you *are* a private investigator."

I smiled and shook my head. "I just wrapped up some work for an insurance company, but that's it." I stared down the street at Shirley's little two-story. "I don't know anything about her." Except that she was a crotchety woman.

"Deuce and I have tried to be nice to her, but she treats us like we're criminals even though we've never done anything to her, or anyone else." Ace's face twisted up in frustration.

I crossed my arms. It was unusual for someone not to like the Goofballs. That said a lot about Shirley, and none of it good.

"Whenever I come home from work, that's about the time she's out taking a walk." Deuce used his construction hardhat to point to her house. He'd just gotten off work about the same time he did every day. "She rarely has anything nice to say."

I pursed my lips. "Where's she from?"

"I heard she moved up here from Texas," Deuce said.

"What'd she do for work?" I asked, imagining Shirley as the stereotypical spinster schoolmarm.

Ace shrugged. "I don't know."

"I think she was a teacher," Deuce said with a knowing nod.

The image was correct, I thought.

3

"She has a granddaughter that lives here in Denver," Deuce went on, "but I don't know if Shirley's close to her."

Ace stared at him in surprise. "How do you know that?"

"A while back I saw a woman with long brown hair coming out of Shirley's house. I said hello and she got in her car and left."

"Then how did you know who she was?" Ace asked pointedly.

"I asked Mr. McCulloch, who lives next door to Shirley. He told me that it was Shirley's granddaughter. And he told me a little bit about her."

"Ah," Ace said, mystery explained. He looked at me. "We're going to B 52s. You want to join us?"

"That sounds like fun," I said.

B 52s is a local bar that we like to go to. I love it because its décor is of a bygone era, with old advertising posters from the '40s and '50s and plane propellers on the walls. They also play '80s music, my favorite. The Goofballs love it because the bar has a back room with pool tables. Both brothers are born pool players, and they beat me most of the time.

"Oh." I snapped my fingers. "Willie and I have to go to that neighborhood meeting tonight."

Ace jerked his head down the street. "The one Shirley mentioned?"

I nodded.

"Have there been problems around here?" Deuce asked.

"Someone's been breaking into some cars and homes," I said. "And there's been an increase in the homeless population. We just want to make sure the neighborhood stays safe.

"Bob may go to the meeting," Ace said. "And he's coming to B 52s afterward."

Bob was the Goofballs' older, and wiser, brother. He'd lived on the East Coast for a while, but several years ago had moved back to Colorado to keep an eye on his younger brothers. He's an EMT, and works odd hours, but he stops by whenever he can.

"Okay," I said. "When the meeting's over, Willie and I might come over for a while."

Deuce smiled. "Cool."

Just then, my wife Willie – real name Willemena – walked around the side of the building and up to us.

"Hi, Willie," the Goofballs said.

"Hi, guys." Willie sidled up next to me and gave me a quick kiss, her green eyes dancing. She gestured at Deuce's hardhat. "Just get home from work?"

"Some detective you are," Deuce said with a laugh.

She punched his arm. "Oh, good one."

Ace pointed to the Best Buy logo on his shirt. "Me, too." Ace is an assistant manager at a nearby store. He knows a lot about electronics, so it's the perfect fit for him.

"I can see that," Willie said. She gave him a light tap on the arm, then ran a hand over her purple hospital shirt. "I just came from work, too." Willie's an ER admissions nurse and works at St. Joe's Hospital. "What're we talking about?"

"Shirley Durocher." Ace's voice dropped.

Willie shivered. "She's kind of a cold woman, isn't she?"

We all agreed.

"Both of us try to be nice to her, but she just frowns at us," Deuce said.

"That's not right," Willie said. "If the two of you can't make friends with someone, there's something wrong with that person, not the two of you."

Willie adored the Goofballs, and the feeling was mutual. They blushed. We all started up the sidewalk to the porch of our building.

"See you later," Willie said.

We waved at the Goofballs, then I gave Willie a longer kiss as we headed around the side of the building to metal stairs that led up to our condo.

"How was your day?" I asked.

"It was busy, and I'm tired. I'd love to take a shower and watch some TV."

"We have that neighborhood meeting tonight."

She groaned. "Oh, that's right."

"I can go by myself if you want," I said as I unlocked our door.

"No, I want to hear what they have to say. Oh, hello." She bent down and picked up a black kitten, held him up to her face, and gave him a kiss. Then she turned him around in her hands and examined him while he meowed loudly. "I think Humphrey's gaining weight, don't you?"

I gazed into his big green eyes. "Yeah, the little runt is getting bigger."

She pulled him toward her chest. "He's not a runt," she said in mock offense. Humphrey batted at her hands. "Goodness, he has a lot of energy."

I shut the door, then reached out and scratched Humphrey's head. "He's my competition for your affections."

"Don't worry." Willie patted my cheek, then stifled a yawn. "Boy, am I tired," she repeated.

"Tell you what. I'll fix some dinner while you shower and change."

"That sounds great."

She gave me a long and lingering kiss, and I pulled her close.

"Or, we can both skip the meeting," I said huskily.

She pulled away. "Later, okay?"

She handed Humphrey to me. Then I watched as she headed down the hall to our bedroom.

Hey, I had to try, right?

glasses, a hand cupped to his ear. Mr. Darmody turned to look at Shirley.

Prestwick blinked slowly a few times. "What do you propose we do?"

"Cut down the trees."

The blinking continued. "Which trees?" he finally said.

"All of them."

"Shirley ..." Prestwick cleared his throat. "These are old, stately trees. I can't imagine cutting them down. And I can't ask the individual homeowners to do something like that."

"You should at least expect them to clean up better," she snapped. "I do my part."

"I'm sure everyone is trying to do their best," Prestwick said.

"Their best isn't good enough." She put her hands on her hips.

"Listen, lady," Phil began, but Prestwick put a hand on his arm.

"I want it put in the notes that there's been a request for tree mitigation," Shirley said.

"I'll make note of it." The frown on Mrs. Johansen's face told exactly what she thought about having to type out the request.

"Thank you," Shirley said snippily.

Prestwick started to say the meeting was adjourned, but Shirley held up a hand. Prestwick sighed.

"I also want an accounting of what our monthly dues are paying for," she said.

Several years back, some industrious folks had banded together to start a Homeowners Association. I wasn't a big fan of HOAs, but I had to admit that, for the most part, our association had done a good job of keeping the neighborhood nice. Many of the buildings in the neighborhood used the same management company, which oversaw things like exterior painting and snow removal, and I hadn't heard of any issues with the job the management company was doing.

"Shirley," Prestwick began. "I provided you with a list of expenses."

"I know you did, but I don't think that was correct."

Phil stood up. "I can assure you that it's all correct, and I can pass along detailed information, if need be."

"There are discrepancies." She waved a hand to encompass us all. "You need to be aware that there's something fishy going on."

"Shirley," Phil said angrily. "That is not the case. I am an accountant and–"

"Don't you talk to me that way," she interrupted. "I am telling you something is not right." She pointed at Phil. "You are stealing from us, and we're going to get to the bottom of this."

Shirley, Phil, and Prestwick continued to argue while Mrs. Johansen sat with pursed lips. Willie leaned over to me.

"Have you heard about any of this?"

I shook my head. "But if Phil's an accountant, wouldn't he have the numbers correct?"

"On the other hand, if anyone would know how to get something illegal past us, he would."

"Good point," I muttered.

"What's more," Shirley was saying, her finger still pointed at Phil, "I think I've seen you around my house late at night. You know I'm on to you, and you're trying to scare me off."

My ears perked up at that. She'd also accused the Goofballs of spying on her. Was it her imagination, or had someone been sneaking around her house? The neighborhood thief?

Phil put a hand on his chest. "That is so far from the truth, I am deeply offended. I don't know what to say."

Prestwick held up a big hand. "Shirley, we can discuss this later, when you have facts to substantiate your claims."

"Oh, I do," she said, but she sat down and crossed her arms.

Prestwick adjusted his tie again. "Does anyone have anything else they'd like to address?"

The room remained silent, so Prestwick adjourned the meeting. Chairs scraped the floor as people stood up and moved toward the door. Shirley stomped quickly out of the room.

Bob got up and stretched. "That was exciting."

I grinned. "For once, it actually was. I've never seen anyone get riled up at one of these meetings."

He scratched his chin. "Do you think there's truth to the accounting issue?"

"I haven't heard that before."

He nodded. "Let me know if you find out anything."

Bob and I helped fold up some chairs, and then he said, "I'm headed to B 52s. You two coming?"

I looked at Willie. "What do you think?"

"I was tired earlier, but I've got a second wind. Let's go for a little while."

"Great," Bob said. "I'll see you over there." He headed for the door.

Willie gestured toward the table at the front. "I need to talk to Mrs. Johansen."

"I need to use the restroom, and I'll meet you outside."

I left her and used the facilities, then went outside. The October air was cool and crisp. Darkness had fallen, and I tried to glimpse some stars, but none were out yet. I walked slowly along the side of the building, killing time. When I neared the corner, I heard voices raised in anger.

"I know exactly what you're up to." It was Shirley. She was just as angry as she'd been inside.

"I can assure you, I've been board president for two terms now, and there have never been any issues." This from Alan Prestwick.

"If you want to cover up for Phil Epstein, you can try, but I'm not going to put up with this nonsense. My money is valuable, and if I have to get the law involved, or more, I will. This is important, and if you don't do something about it, I might talk to people. And that won't help you with that other situation."

"You wouldn't do that!"

"If I have to, I will. How would you like that?"

"Don't you threaten me." Prestwick's voice had grown ominous. "You think I don't have ways to handle people like you?"

"That sounds like a threat, too. You better watch yourself."

A crack sounded loudly in the darkness, and Prestwick cleared his throat. Then footsteps clapped on the pavement. I pressed against the wall, but neither one of them came by me. I peeked around the corner. No one was there.

What was that crack? Had one of them hit the other?

I peered into the night and mulled things over. Shirley was certainly stirring things up. Was it justified? The investigator in me didn't think I could let it go, but I hadn't heard anything about the HOA's financials being off. However, I hadn't been at too many meetings.

"You ready to go, hon?"

I jumped at the sound of Willie's voice. She laughed and put her arm on my shoulder.

"I didn't mean to scare you."

"It's okay. I didn't hear you come up behind me."

She looked around the corner. "What's going on? Is there a ghost out there?"

"Nothing." I told her what I'd overheard.

"Do you think Shirley has uncovered something illegal?"

"I don't know, but I'll make a few calls."

"Okay. Let's go."

We walked to my 4-Runner and drove to B 52s. I didn't think about Shirley for the rest of the evening. After a few games of pool, Willie and I headed home.

The next morning, Humphrey Bogart's voice woke me from a deep sleep.

"The cheaper the crook, the gaudier the patter."

It was a new sound bite I'd installed, Humphrey Bogart in *The Maltese Falcon*. I'm an avid film noir fan. I love those movies with the dark, noir hero and the femme fatales. And I aspire to be as cool as Bogie was. A stretch, I know, but I can dream, can't I?

Willie mumbled something about killing whoever was calling so early as I picked up my phone. I recognized the number. Deuce.

"What's up, buddy?" I said through a yawn.

"You're never going to believe it."

"What?"

Humphrey – the kitten – jumped up on my chest and began purring.

"Shirley Durocher's dead."

CHAPTER THREE

"What happened?" I set Humphrey next to me, sat up, and rubbed my eyes with my free hand. Humphrey meowed and tried to bat at my face, and I played with him while I talked.

"I don't know," Deuce said. "There were some people standing on the sidewalk near her house, and when I drove by to go to work, I saw Mr. Darmody, so I waved him over. He came over, and we started talking, and he asked me if I'd heard the news. So I said 'what news?' And he told me. I've got to get to work, but I thought I'd let you know."

I was getting the long, drawn-out version.

"Wow," I said.

Willie rolled over. "What's the matter?" she asked through a yawn.

I angled the phone away from my mouth. "Shirley Durocher is dead."

"I know that," Deuce said.

I put the phone back to my mouth. "I was telling Willie."

"Oh."

I could picture Deuce blushing.

Willie was awake now. "What happened?"

She grabbed Humphrey and scratched him behind his ears. He closed his eyes, and I swear I could hear him sigh contentedly.

I shrugged at her, and repeated to Deuce, "What happened to Shirley?"

"I don't know, but I think the police are there. I saw your friend, that detective lady, on the porch. She was talking to a couple of other guys who looked like cops."

"Spillman," I said.

"Yeah," Deuce replied. "That's her."

It was funny hearing Deuce call Sarah Spillman my friend. She's a homicide detective with the Denver Police Department, and I've run into her on numerous cases of mine. She usually accuses me of interfering in her investigations, and I always deny it – whether it's true or not – but over time she's realized I am a decent private investigator. Because of that, she isn't afraid to help me out now and then. She's met Willie and the Goofballs, and she even attended our wedding. If Spillman was at Shirley's house, it meant the death was suspicious.

I rubbed my jaw. "Huh."

"What?" Willie whispered.

"Spillman's over there," I said.

"I just told you that," Deuce said.

"I was talking to Willie again."

"Oh. Hey, I gotta go," Deuce said. "I've got to call Ace and tell him about this."

"Okay, talk to you later."

I put my phone back on the nightstand.

"What're you going to do?" Willie asked.

I rolled over and propped up on an elbow. "What do you mean?"

"Are you going to talk to Spillman and find out what happened?"

"I guess I could."

"Aren't you the least bit curious?"

I shrugged. "I don't know."

She eyed me suspiciously. "You're not fooling me. You're dying to find out what happened."

I grinned. "Yeah, I am." I slid out from under the covers and Humphrey leaped off the bed. He found his toy mouse on the floor and began playing with it, batting it in the air and then chasing it. "I'll go over there and find out what I can."

"I'll let you do the investigating while I take a shower, and I've got to get to work."

I stepped over Humphrey. "I'll beat you to the shower," I said on my way to the bathroom.

"Not fair, you were already up."

I laughed, then took a very quick shower and threw on jeans and a shirt. I kissed her on my way out of the bedroom, then went outside and down the stairs. By the time I'd reached the sidewalk, I saw some neighbors milling about down the street. The sun was still low in the sky, and a chill filled the air as I headed toward them. Then I saw a blue '65 Mustang parked at the curb in front of Shirley's house. Spillman's car. A silver sedan was parked in front of the Mustang, but I didn't see a morgue vehicle.

"Do you know what's going on?" Mr. Darmody asked. He was an octogenarian who lived next door to me. His wife tugged at her sweater and gave me a nervous smile.

"I don't," I replied. "What have you heard?"

He pursed his lips. "Nothing."

I glanced past him. Partway up the walk that led to Shirley's front porch were two men in conversation. Roland Youngfield – nicknamed "Spats" because he liked to dress well – lived up to his handle with a tailored gray suit, complete with vest and tie. The other man – Ernie Moore – was the stereotypical detective in a rumpled brown suit and no tie. They were Spillman's partners, and I'd run into them a few times as well.

Both eyed me cautiously as I approached. Unlike Spillman, they were not particularly fond of me. Moore gave me a curt nod, and Youngfield sized me up.

"What're you doing here?" Moore grunted.

"I live down the street." Then I pointed at the house. "I know ... knew ... Shirley Durocher."

"Oh yeah?" Moore stared at me.

Moore should've remembered where I lived. He and Spats had driven me home one time, after I'd stopped a killer from murdering one of Denver's better-known businessmen. Or maybe he was just giving me a hard time.

"You're not working on a case that involves this poor woman, are you?" a low, feminine voice asked.

I looked up to see Detective Spillman standing on Shirley's front porch, her hands on her hips. In her khaki slacks, green-striped blouse, and tan blazer, she could've been going to an office, not working a homicide investigation. Except for the latex gloves and booties covering her shoes.

I held up my hands in mock defense. "I live down the street."

"And that naturally makes you curious." She glanced behind me at the gawkers. "I wondered when you would show up, asking questions."

"I guess I'm that predictable."

She nodded, and then her eyes narrowed. "You're really not involved with any of this?" She waved a hand behind her.

I shook my head. "No. But since I'm the neighborhood private investigator, folks think I should be able to glean some information from you."

"Uh-huh."

I waited a second. "Can you tell me anything?"

She gave my neighbors another brief look, and then gestured at me to come up onto the porch.

"You can't come inside, and you can't tell the neighbors anything."

"Don't worry, I won't." I jerked a thumb behind me. "Has her body been taken to the morgue?"

"A little while ago." She turned her back to the street and went on. "She was discovered by Roberto Bonifacio."

I arched an eyebrow. "From a few doors down?"

"You know him?"

"I've seen him around, but haven't talked to him much, just a hello here or there. His wife passed away a few years ago, and he keeps to himself. Why would he have discovered Shirley?"

"Apparently they've been seeing one another."

I stared at her. "You're kidding."

She tipped her head. "You weren't aware of that?"

I shook my head. I thought back to yesterday, when I'd seen Shirley pass by Mr. Bonifacio's house.

"The last time I saw them," I said, "they didn't seem friendly with each other."

"According to Bonifacio," she said, "they would get together a couple of times a week."

"Get together?"

She tipped her head. "You know what I mean. They tried to keep it quiet."

"I guess so," I murmured.

"Bonifacio came over this morning to have an early breakfast with Mrs. Durocher."

"Who? Oh, Shirley." I smiled wanly.

"Anyway, Bonifacio let himself in with a key and found Mrs. Durocher in the kitchen. The side of her head took a blow."

"That killed her?"

She shrugged. "That, or it caused her to have a heart attack. I won't know until after the autopsy."

I held up a hand. "If you're here, you don't think it was an accident."

"I don't know what we have just yet."

I glanced toward Bonifacio's house. "You think he had anything to do with her death?"

Her eyes bore into me. "You're sure you're not investigating this?"

"Nope."

It took her a moment to answer. "I can't tell you about any potential suspects, but nothing he said aroused my suspicions." She drew in a breath. "It's too early to tell about much of anything."

"Fair enough."

"Tell me about Mr. Bonifacio."

I shrugged. "He's friendly when I see him. I think he was a teacher. But that's about it."

"What about your other neighbors? Anyone have any problems with Mrs. Durocher?"

"Not that I'm aware of."

"What did you know about Mrs. Durocher?" she asked.

"Not a whole lot. She's lived around here for a long time, but I haven't had a lot of interaction with her."

"Tell me about the encounters you *did* have."

I hesitated. "I hate to speak ill about the dead, but she wasn't the nicest person."

"Kind of a crotchety old woman?"

"You could say that." I gave her an example of the encounter Ace, Deuce, and I'd had with her. "If those two can't make friends with her, you have to wonder about her."

Spillman laughed. "That's true." She ran a hand through her blond hair. "Anything else about her?"

"She has a daughter, and a granddaughter, but I've never met either of them. Deuce met the granddaughter, but I don't think he mentioned her name."

"I found some paperwork for the daughter, and we'll be contacting her. So the granddaughter lives in town?"

I shrugged. "Or she came from out of town for a visit."

"You don't have any idea if Mrs. Durocher was close to her family?"

"I don't."

"Was she divorced or did her husband die?"

"I don't know. Deuce said she was from Texas." I crossed my arms. "I suspect you know more about her than I do."

She nodded. "Spats and Moore will be working on it. I should talk to Ace and Deuce."

"To be honest, they'd probably get nervous and have a hard time telling you anything."

She thought about that. "Maybe you can be there, help to relax them."

"I can do that."

She glanced inside the front door. I did, too, curious to glean something about Shirley from how she decorated her house.

"Who might've wanted to kill Mrs. Durocher?" Spillman asked.

"That's a good question."

"I thought so."

I chuckled. "The only thing that comes to mind is last night. We had a neighborhood meeting, and she was pretty upset with Phil Epstein and Alan Prestwick." I told Spillman about Shirley's suspicions that Epstein had cooked the accounting books, and about her argument after the meeting with Prestwick. "I don't know what she meant about the trouble Prestwick was in."

"Interesting." She didn't write anything down, but I was sure she'd remember everything I'd just said.

"Oh." I held up a hand. "And she was worried that someone might be watching her house at night."

"Who?"

I shrugged again. "I don't know. We've had some problems with break-ins, and some homeless people have been in the alleys, but I don't know if anyone was watching Shirley's house specifically."

"Did you notice anything suspicious last night?"

I shook my head. "No. Willie and I left the meeting and went to B 52s, and nothing was unusual when we came home."

A faint smile crossed her face. "You don't know much of anything, do you?"

I gave her a grin of my own. "Not really, but as I said, it's not my investigation." I winked. "It's yours."

"Touché." She looked around again. "If you hear anything else, give me a call."

"Absolutely."

I wished her the best, turned around, and headed down the sidewalk. Spats and Moore were talking to some of the onlookers, but both eyed me again as I walked past them.

Mr. Darmody waved me over. "What'd you find out?"

"I don't have any answers," I said.

"Is the neighborhood safe?" Mrs. Darmody asked, her voice so quiet I barely heard her.

"We need to keep a lookout for anything suspicious," I said, "but at this point, I don't think you need to be extra worried."

"Yes, okay," she said.

"We always keep an eye out," Mr. Darmody added.

"Good."

I thanked them and headed back toward my building. Willie was outside, talking to her best friend, Darcy Cranston. Darcy, an attractive African-American woman with dark eyes and a killer sense of humor, lived across the street in one of the apartments in the Victorian house that Willie owns.

"What'd you find out?" Willie asked.

I told them what little I'd learned.

"Do you think it has to do with the burglaries in the neighborhood?" they asked at once.

"I don't know. Spillman didn't know a whole lot, either, or she wasn't sharing. We'll have to see where this all goes."

"It's a little strange that you're not working this case, isn't it?" Darcy said.

"Yeah, but I'll leave this one for Spillman."

As it turned out, that's not where it went at all.

CHAPTER FOUR

A week went by, and shortly before noon on a cloudy Tuesday, a knock sounded on my door. I opened it and Cal Whitmore entered. My best friend since grade school, Cal's practically a member of the family.

"What's up, O Great Detective?" he said in his nasally voice.

This is Cal's standard greeting for me, no matter how much I try to talk him out of it.

"How'd your meeting go?" I asked.

He set his backpack down near the door. It was partially open and Humphrey immediately crawled inside, but Cal didn't notice. Cal is a computer geek who runs his own cyber-security consulting company out of his home near Pine Junction in the foothills southwest of Denver. He lives like a hermit, rarely leaving his house, unless he has to meet a client in town. When he does, we try to get together.

"This company needs a lot of work," he said. "It's going to be a challenging contract."

"I have no doubt you're up to the task."

I meant it. Cal is brilliant, although like many geniuses, he has little common sense.

Cal had bent down and was wrestling Humphrey from the backpack. "I still don't understand what you see in this cat," he said.

"It's not your thing." I grinned. "But you have to admit he's cute."

"I don't know about that."

Humphrey meowed as Cal finally extracted him from the backpack.

"Oh, you like that?" Cal cooed at him. "You stay out of my stuff, you hear?"

"You can't fool me. You're just a softy."

Cal glanced up and rolled his eyes. "Where do you want to go for lunch?"

"How about–"

Another knock on the door interrupted me. Now Cal cocked an eyebrow.

"Is someone else joining us?"

I shook my head. "No. Willie's at work, and I didn't invite anyone else."

I crossed to the door and opened it. Ace stood there with a woman with long brown hair whom I didn't recognize.

"Hi, Reed," he said with a wave. "Um, do you have a minute?"

"Sure." I glanced from him to the woman, then back to Ace.

"Uhn-uh, you stay with me," Cal said behind me.

I assumed he had picked up Humphrey so he wouldn't go outside.

Ace jerked a finger at the woman. "This is Holly Durocher." The name wasn't ringing any bells, and Ace astutely noticed that. "She's Shirley's granddaughter."

"Oh, okay." I reached out and shook Holly's hand. "It's nice to meet you. I'm so sorry about your grandmother." I gauged her to be in her mid-thirties.

"Thanks." She barely made eye contact before she looked back at Ace.

"I ran into Holly down the street, and I told her about how you're a detective," Ace said, "and how you might be able to help her."

She was still having a hard time making eye contact. She fiddled with the hem of her untucked yellow blouse.

I looked at Holly. "What do you need help with?"

She finally glanced up at me. "Well ..." she hesitated.

"I'm sorry," I said. "Why don't you come in?"

I stepped back and let them into the condo. Holly stopped short when she saw Cal. Cal had been petting Humphrey, but he set him on the floor and stared at Holly, then gave her a shy smile. She relaxed for just a moment and returned his smile.

I glanced between them. What was that about? I introduced them, and she shook his hand.

"This is Cal Whitmore. Cal's my best friend," I said, "but if you'd like, I'm sure he wouldn't mind going into my office while we talk."

Before she could reply, Ace said, "Cal helps with Reed's investigations, along with Deuce and me."

I stared at Ace in surprise. He was trying to impress her.

"I don't mind if you stay," Holly said to Cal.

"Thanks."

Now I was surprised with Cal. "You sure you want to hear this?"

"Of course."

Cal sat down at the end of the couch, and Holly sank into a recliner. I perched on the other end of the couch near her, and Ace leaned against the wall by the TV stand. Humphrey played with a little ball, oblivious to us.

Holly put her hands in her lap. The fiddling with her blouse hem continued. "Cute kitten," she said.

"His name is Humphrey," Cal replied. "As in Humphrey Bogart."

She nodded. "That's nice."

Silence filled the room. I was about to say something when she began.

"I ran into Ace outside. I'd come to my grandmother's house to take care of a few things, and we got to talking." She glanced over at Ace.

"It's okay," he nudged her. "You can trust Reed."

He was being so kind and gentle with her, it was heart-warming.

"I'm in trouble," she said.

"What's going on?" I asked.

She let out a sigh that carried a huge burden with it. "I'm pretty sure the police think I had something to do with my grandmother's death."

"Why would the police suspect you?"

"Because she left me all of her money. If you include the house, almost a million dollars."

Cal whistled. I glanced over at him, and he shrugged naively. "It's a lot of money," he murmured.

"Yes, it is," I said, then turned to Cal and gave him a "be quiet" look. He was showing more interest in this woman than I'd seen him show anyone in a long time. I turned back to Holly. Ace seemed to get the idea, too, and he pressed his lips shut and let Holly and me talk.

"You're right," she went on. "And I can see why the police would think I might murder for that kind of money. But I didn't do it."

"Okay," I said. "Do you have an alibi?"

She shook her head. "I was home alone. I ordered Chinese

for dinner, watched some TV, and went to bed. So no way to prove I didn't visit my grandmother the night she died. Not only that, my mother – Shirley's daughter, obviously – is accusing me of having my grandmother's will changed, or switching an old will to this most recent one."

"Your mother told the police that?"

"I don't know that for sure, but I suspect she did. Mom told me what she thought about the wills when she found out she wasn't inheriting anything. And she was mad enough that she wasn't getting anything that I could see her telling the police that."

"Are you aware of another will?"

She shook her head. "I didn't even know about this one. My grandmother never told me what she planned to do when she died. I was surprised when the attorney called and said she'd left everything to me. And like I said, Mom is furious. She thinks she was supposed to get the inheritance, not me."

"When was the will dated?"

"Several years ago."

Holly was right that the police would take a close look at her, with that kind of money at stake. But what about Holly's mother? The police would look at her, too. It was a process of elimination, checking the most likely suspects first. And that was usually family.

"Is your father around?"

"No. They divorced when I was a baby, and I never knew him."

"Wait." I held up a hand. "You all have the same last name."

She smiled. "My mother and grandmother are independent women, and they kept their maiden names."

I nodded. "How well do you get along with your mother?" I asked, figuring I could guess the answer. But I wanted to hear what she had to say.

31

"We're not close. Mom resents the fact that I've done well for myself. I own a little cupcake shop in Golden. Sunshine Cupcakes. It does well for me. I haven't gotten married yet, and I don't have kids. It's just me and the shop right now. I'm not rich, but I do all right. Which is kind of funny. I don't need the money my grandmother left me. Anyway, Mom is jealous of me, and jealous that I got along better with my grandmother than she did. That made Mom mad, too."

"Your mom and grandmother didn't like each other much?"

She shook her head again. "As Grandmother grew older, I think she realized that her family was important, and that's why she wanted to get together with me more."

"But not your mom?"

She snorted. "Let's face it. My grandmother wasn't the easiest person to get along with." Her head dropped. "Grandmother tried to mend fences, but Mom wouldn't have any of that."

"What caused the rift between Shirley and your mother?"

Her shoulders went up ever so slightly and back down. "I don't know. Mom didn't talk about it. When I was little, we moved up to Denver and I didn't have a lot of contact with Grandmother. I'd go back to Texas, but never to see my grandmother. Mom said she didn't want that nasty woman around me. That's all she'd say." She frowned. "My grandmother can be a very demanding person, she wants things a certain way. It was difficult for Mom to live up to those expectations. She didn't go to college, but got married young and then divorced. None of that made Grandmother happy, and Mom hated her for that. Then Grandmother moved up here, and Mom didn't like that, either."

"And yet your mom thought she'd get an inheritance."

"Yeah, that's my mom."

"What does your mother do?"

"She's retired now. She's gone from job to job, and never saved much. She lives on her Social Security. It's not much, and she's barely squeaking by. I've had to help her out here and there."

I thought for a moment. "Do you know who might've wanted to murder your grandmother? Did she have any enemies?"

She let out another snort. "You knew her, right?"

I nodded.

"She didn't make friends well." Sadness swept across her face. "In all seriousness, I don't know. My grandmother kept to herself, and I don't know much of what she did, or how she kept herself busy, other than her garden."

"Did you know about her relationship with Mr. Bonifacio?"

"Who?"

Ace piped up. "He lives two houses down from her."

She glanced at him, then back at me. "Does he wear thick glasses?"

"Yes," I said.

"Oh, Bert. I saw him once when I came over to visit. I'd come unannounced, and when Grandmother answered the door, he let himself out. They didn't seem overly pleasant with each other."

"Maybe she had him leave because you showed up," I said. "Maybe they didn't want you to know what was going on, so they kept their interaction cool."

"That could be." She gnawed her lip. "But would he have a reason to murder her?"

That hung in the air for a moment.

"I don't know," I finally said. "Tell me what you can about Shirley and her past."

"I don't know much. She grew up in Texas, got married there, then divorced the guy. I never met my grandfather, and what little she said about him wasn't good. He was a bum who disappeared on her." She tapped the arm of the recliner. "She was a schoolteacher. I don't know who her friends were or anything like that. I got a phone call now and then from her, and when she retired, she suddenly announced that she was going to move up here to be closer to me. I thought that was a nice thing, although since she can be difficult, I was a little worried about it. But I figured let the past be the past, and I'd help her out if I could."

"That's very nice of you," Cal said, looking directly at Holly.

"We should look out for one another, don't you think?" She smiled shyly at him.

"Oh, yeah, that's so true," Cal went on.

I glanced at him, but he ignored me. I shifted, trying to catch his eye, wondering what he was doing. This was highly unusual behavior for him.

Holly threw me pleading eyes. "I don't know what went on with my grandmother, but she didn't deserve this. I don't have a lot of money, but Ace said you might be able to help me. I want to clear my name with the police, but more importantly, I want justice for Grandmother. Will you help me?"

Before I could reply, Cal said, "Reed'll be happy to look into your grandmother's death, and I will, too."

I stared at Cal again and narrowed my eyes. He looked at me as if to say "What?" I couldn't believe this was coming from the man who barely interacts with anybody. But the truth is, he and I do make a good team. Think Sherlock Holmes and Dr. Watson, except that Cal should really be Holmes because Cal's way smarter than I am. And his internet wizardry makes my professional life easier, since he can access information that's not publicly available – don't ask me how – and he finds information much faster than I can. But that doesn't mean he can just offer up our services to strangers as he was doing now.

Holly breathed a sigh of relief. "That'd be great."

"What?" I looked back at Holly and refocused. Then I named my fee. "Is that suitable for you?"

"Yes, that'll work."

Ace beamed at me. "You're on the case." He turned to Holly. "Reed's a great detective, and this'll be an easy case for him."

I hoped I'd live up to his assessment.

CHAPTER FIVE

"Let me have you sign some paperwork," I said to Holly.

I took her back to my office. Ace and Cal followed and crowded into the doorway while Holly stood near my desk. She looked around at all my first-edition books, my collection of old movies, and then her eyes fell on my most prized possessions: rare framed posters of *The Maltese Falcon* and *The Big Sleep*, both with Bogie, and *The Postman Always Rings Twice*, with Lana Turner and John Garfield.

"Cool posters," Holly said.

I smiled as I sat down and reached into a desk drawer for my contracts. "I'm a film noir buff. *The Postman Always Rings Twice* is my favorite."

"His wife gave him that," Ace said, "as a wedding present."

Holly glanced at him. "That's sweet."

"You like those movies?" Cal asked.

"Sure. The noir heroes, the dangerous women. What's not to like?" She turned fire-engine red. "They're so not me," she murmured.

"Of course not," Cal said.

I stared at him. He shrugged. I filled in some blanks on the paperwork, then pushed the papers across the desk.

"Read that, and then sign at the bottom," I said to Holly.

She nodded, read the paperwork, then took a pen from me and signed the contract. I got her contact information, and then we all traipsed back into the living room.

"I'd like to talk to your mom, if she'll see me," I said. "Where does she live?"

"She's got a small house in Green Mountain." Holly gave me the address, and I grabbed a pad and pen from the end table and wrote it down. "She's been there for a long time. She's going to freak when she finds out I hired a private investigator."

"I'll try not to let her know."

"She'll figure it out."

"Do you want to call her before I stop by?"

She shook her head. "No way."

So the confrontation was left to me. Well, I could handle it.

"Reed'll have the element of surprise," Cal interjected. "That's the way a private eye works."

I stared at him again, but he was looking at Holly.

"What's your mother's name?" I asked her.

"Karen Durocher."

"I've got your phone number," I went on. "What's hers?"

She had to look it up on her cell phone. I wrote it down as well.

"Give me a day or two to make some inquiries," I said, "and I'll call you with an update."

"That's great." Holly moved toward the door. "I'm working at the shop, but I can take calls any time. I want to get to the bottom of this as fast as we can."

I nodded. "That's my goal, too."

Ace had been standing near the door, and he opened it. "I'll go downstairs with you."

"That'd be nice." She smiled at him and it was his turn to blush.

Ace turned to me. "I offered to help her get some of Shirley's food into the car."

"I'm clearing out things in the refrigerator," Holly explained. "I don't want anything to go bad."

I raised my eyebrows. "Your grandmother's house isn't a crime scene anymore?"

She shook her head. "They wrapped up last night and said I could go back in the house." She pursed her lips. "It's going to take some time to go through her things and get the place ready to sell."

"Take your time," Cal said. "You want a clear head when you make financial decisions."

She looked at him. "That's good advice."

I gestured at the door. "Would you mind if I looked around her house?"

She shrugged. "You think you might find something that would lead to her murderer?"

"I might," I said.

"Okay, sure."

She followed Ace outside, and I went after them, with Cal at my heels.

"Since when are you so interested in a case of mine?" I whispered over my shoulder.

"It sounds interesting," he murmured.

I turned and gave him a curious look.

"Hurry up." He nudged me onto the landing.

"Don't let Humphrey out," I said.

He nodded, scolded the kitten to stay, then shut the door. Ace and Holly had reached the bottom of the stairs, and they disappeared around the corner. Ace was chattering at Holly about how he had helped me in the past, but I didn't hear

Holly's voice. Cal and I joined them on the front porch, and we walked down the block to Shirley's house. Holly unlocked the door and we all went inside.

"Where was your grandmother found?" Cal gently asked Holly.

"In the kitchen," she said, pointing past the living room to the left of the door.

"Really?" Ace stood in the foyer, his hands rubbing up and down his arms. "Maybe I should stay here." His gaze darted toward the kitchen.

Holly looked at him and suddenly realized he was nervous. "Sure, that's no problem. If you want. Maybe Cal can help me take things to the car."

"Sure," Cal said.

Ace tried to look cool, but it was obvious he didn't want to be where Shirley had died. "Yeah, okay. If you think that's all right."

"It is."

"Is it okay, Reed?" he whispered at me.

I patted his shoulder. "It's fine. Why don't you go on home? If I need your help with the case, I'll let you know." I said that last part loud enough so that Holly heard.

Ace squared his shoulders importantly, waved at her, and stepped outside.

"He's sweet," Holly said.

"Yes, he is," I agreed.

She motioned for me to follow her into the kitchen. It was small, not too many cabinets, with a sink under a window that looked out into a tiny back yard. Shirley's style leaned toward country kitchen, with lots of cutesy farm animals on her dish towels and in little pictures hung on the walls. The room was neat and orderly, with no visible signs that she had died here.

THE DAMNED DON'T DIE

Cal looked around, then leaned against the wall near a small round table and chairs in the corner so Holly and I could talk.

"They found her near there." She pointed at the sink. "She was lying on her side, and she had a gash in her head."

I thought about what Spillman had said. "Any chance it was an accident?"

Holly let out a big breath. "That's not what the police seem to think at this point." Her eyes roved around the room. "They dusted for fingerprints."

"Huh," I said. "The police told you they dusted for fingerprints?" I asked.

"No, I assumed so." She ran a hand subconsciously along the counter. "I wiped the dust away."

I made a mental note to ask Spillman about that. Although since I was now on the case, I wasn't sure what she'd tell me.

"I'm sure they found hers, mine, my mother's, and Bert's," she went on. "Beyond that, I don't know."

I stared at her. "Bert? Oh, Mr. Bonifacio." I thought for a second. "Does anything seem out of the ordinary since the last time you were here?"

She looked at me. "Is anything missing? Is that what you mean?"

I nodded. "Or anything moved?"

"Not that I know of."

"Would your mother know?" I asked.

She shrugged. "I couldn't tell you the last time Mom was here."

I stepped up to the cupboards and opened one. It was full of spices and baking items.

"What do you hope to find?" Holly asked.

"I don't know." I moved toward the doorway and Cal stepped back. "Mind if we look around the rest of the house?"

"Not at all," she said.

41

Cal and I went back into the living room. It was functional, with a couch, a reclining chair that faced a small TV, and an old coffee table. I went to a desk in the corner and opened drawers. There were bills, lined paper, typing paper, pens, papers, and some old letters. Some were signed by Karen, some by someone named Bob, some by other people.

I held them up. "Do you recognize any of these names?"

She stepped up and looked over my shoulder, then took them from me. "They don't mean anything to me."

I put the letters back and looked in the other drawers. In one was a shoebox full of old photos. I picked up a few, which were mostly of Shirley.

"Did you look through these photos? Do you know who these people are?"

"I don't know who that is with Grandmother, but I think she's in front of her house in Texas."

I showed Holly a few more photos, waiting to see if she had any clue who was in them, or where they had been taken, but she remained silent. I finally put the box back.

"I'll go through the desk later today," she said, "and if I find anything that I think you should see, I'll let you know."

"Okay."

We went into the dining room, which had an antique table and chairs, and a hutch with dishes displayed on it. Then we moved on to a spare bedroom, but didn't see anything notewor- thy, so we walked upstairs. There was a little sitting area with a chair and a small table, and a bookcase full of paperbacks. Past that was a small bathroom and the master bedroom, just big enough for a queen-size bed, a dresser, and one nightstand. I glanced around, quickly checked under the bed, in the closet, and then opened the dresser drawers. I didn't want to rifle through Shirley's delicates unless I had to, and I didn't see any reason to now, so I moved to the window. I separated the blinds and looked past the back yard into the alley. A white truck was parked at the end of it, and I thought I caught a glimpse of someone in it.

"Did your grandmother ever talk about someone watching her house?" I asked.

Holly nodded. "Now that you mention it, she did say something about that the last time I was here. I thought she was kidding, just being kind of grumpy like she gets." Her jaw dropped. "You don't think that whoever was watching her killed her?"

I stepped away from the window. "I don't know."

Holly waved a hand around. "I'm not sure what there is to find."

I nodded slowly. "I don't know, either. Why don't we go back downstairs?"

I followed her out of the bedroom, and we ended in the entryway.

"So," Holly said. "Did you find out anything?"

"Your grandmother seemed to keep a tidy household," I said, "and she didn't have a lot of stuff."

She nodded. "There's still plenty to go through."

"I'm sure." Cal's tone was supportive.

I looked around one final time. "I guess that's it. We can help you carry the stuff to the car, if you'd like."

"I'd appreciate it," she said.

Cal and I helped her carry some boxes of groceries to her car, which was parked by the garage at the back of the house. As we loaded them into her back seat and trunk, I caught a glimpse of the white truck again. It wasn't one I recognized. I stared at it for a second.

"That's it," Holly announced as she and Cal put some boxes in the back seat. "Thanks for your help."

"Sure thing," I said. "I'll be in touch soon."

"I look forward to it."

We waited until she got in and drove off, then Cal and I walked back to my building. When we reached the alley entrance to the small yard and garages, I handed Cal the condo keys.

"Let yourself in." I gestured subtly down the alley. "I'll be right back."

"All right."

He went through the gate, and I started down the alley toward the truck. Its engine suddenly roared to life, and it backed into the street and peeled away with squealing tires. I ran after it, but couldn't see who was driving. Except that whoever it was had on a cowboy hat. I reached the corner and stared down the street, but the truck had merged into traffic and was gone. I watched the traffic for a minute, then turned and headed back down the alley.

What was that about? I wondered as I walked back to my building.

CHAPTER SIX

Humphrey trotted to me when I walked inside.

"Hey, buddy," I said as I picked him up.

"I saw what you did at Shirley's house," Cal said.

He was sitting at the kitchen table, his laptop open.

"What's that?"

"When we helped Holly take things to her car, you made sure she didn't take anything significant from her grandmother's house. Like evidence."

I set Humphrey down, and he scampered over to a toy mouse and began batting it up in the air. Then something – I have no idea what – scared him, and he leaped straight up into the air, his little tail puffed up. I chuckled as he ran under the table.

"Unless she smuggled something out with the groceries," I said. "I didn't check that too well."

"Ah, I hadn't thought of that."

"Uh-huh."

I moved over by him and gave him a long look. He stopped typing and stared at me.

"What?" he asked.

"Want to tell me about you and Holly?"

"What do you mean?"

I grinned at him. "You like her."

"I do not."

"There's nothing wrong with that. She's cute."

"Don't be silly. I'm just trying to be helpful." He cleared his throat and focused on the laptop.

"Uh-huh."

He waved a hand at me. "What's your next move, O Great Detective?"

I let him get away with the deflection. "I need to talk to Karen Durocher, but I want to know more about her. And Holly and Shirley, too." I pointed a finger at him. "Feel like helping? You did offer our services to Holly."

"I technically offered *your* services."

I shook my head. "No, it was both of us."

He laughed. "Of course I'll help." He gestured at the screen. "I've already got some searches started."

"You okay if we don't go to lunch?" I asked as I headed toward the kitchen. "I can fix some sandwiches."

"That's fine." He was typing furiously.

I got out bread, mustard, mayo, and some thinly sliced roast beef, and started on the sandwiches. I'd known Cal long enough to know exactly what he wanted on his. I whistled softly while Humphrey played at my feet, and I had to be careful not to step on him.

"Okay, here's what I found," Cal said a few minutes later. "Shirley Durocher was born in Dallas, Texas, in 1939. She was a schoolteacher in Muleshoe for over forty years, and I don't see anything problematic in her record."

"Muleshoe?"

"Yep. It's a little town in the Panhandle. Anyway, Shirley doesn't have a criminal record. I can't even find a speeding ticket. Her finances were in order. She had a retirement with the state, and she did pretty well for herself, taking quite a few cruises."

I whistled loudly. "That had to cost a pretty penny."

"She has a lot of money."

"On a schoolteacher's salary?"

I brought the sandwiches and chips to the table, then grabbed us Cokes. We chatted as we ate our sandwiches.

"Maybe she invested wisely. If you looked around her house, she didn't spend much."

"Interesting."

"I'll spend more time later on her, to see if I can find anything suspicious with her money."

"Good. What about her ex-husband?"

"Ah, now that's interesting." He set down his sandwich and typed for a minute. "I can't find one."

I stared at him. "Really?"

He nodded. "No marriage license that I can find. I can look some more, but nothing comes up right away."

"Huh."

"I also don't find a father for Karen Durocher," he said. "The father's name is not listed on Karen's birth certificate. You want me to dig deeper, see what I can find?"

I shook my head. "If he's not listed, I don't know where we'd find it. You found out a lot as it is."

Humphrey jumped in my lap, curled up, and promptly fell asleep.

"I got lucky with the search." He tapped the monitor. "Some days are good, others not so much."

"What about a death certificate for someone named Durocher?"

He shook his head. "Without a first name, that'd be searching for a needle in a haystack."

"So was this guy a bum who up and left before his daughter was born?"

"Kind of looks that way."

"What about Karen Durocher?"

He took a few more bites of his sandwich, gulped some Coke, and stared at the screen. "Not a whole lot on her either. I don't see any retirement income. Looks like she has a couple of DUIs in her past, nothing recent. She's had a number of jobs over the years, nothing steady. She doesn't have much money. Huh."

"What?"

"She owes a lot on her house."

"So?"

"She bought it in 1985, so it ought to be paid off. Oh, looks like she took out a second mortgage on it, and she's refinanced a time or two, and took money out."

"She could use an inheritance," I said.

He nodded. "All she has is her Social Security, and it's barely paying her mortgage. She's likely struggling, as Holly said."

"What'd she do with the money from the mortgages and re-fis?" I mused.

He shrugged and ate some chips. "I'll see what I can find."

I waited, absentmindedly petting Humphrey, who was dead to the world. That's a kitten for you: play hard, then suddenly sleep hard.

Cal worked at the computer for a while, then said, "I'm not finding anything. I'll need to take some more time to look into this."

"Who was Karen married to?"

"I can't find a marriage license or a birth certificate."

"Karen didn't know her father, and Holly doesn't know hers. Seems to be a pattern. But does it mean anything?"

"I'll see what else I can dig up."

"Hmm," I held up a finger. "Holly said her parents were married, and her grandparents."

"Maybe that's what she was told. And I didn't say that her mother or grandmother weren't married, just that I couldn't find marriage licenses."

I mulled that over. "It's still interesting." I sat back. "What if Shirley and Karen lied about their husbands, and they were boyfriends, not husbands?"

"So?"

"Or Holly's lying. She told me her parents and grandparents were married, even though she knew they weren't."

"She wouldn't do that."

"Oh?"

He shrugged. "Call it a gut feeling."

I grinned.

"What?"

"You do like her."

He didn't say anything to that.

"You've searched on Holly, too, right?" I asked.

"Yes. It's like she told you. She has the cupcake shop in Golden, and it seems to do pretty well for her."

"Who knew there was money in cupcakes?"

"She doesn't have a record of any kind, and her finances are in order."

"She's never been married?"

"Nope."

Was there a bit of hope in his tone? It was fascinating. The man who wasn't interested in women had a crush on a woman.

He finished his chips, then downed his Coke. "What's your next move?"

"I'll talk to Karen Durocher first, and see what she has to say. Then I'll go from there."

"All right." He wiped his hands on his napkin, then shut down his laptop. "I need to head home. I've got work to do, but I'll do some more poking around on these ladies and let you know what I find."

"Perfect. Oh, just one more thing."

"You sound like Columbo, from the TV show. Always one more thing."

"There's always one more thing. Look up Phil Epstein. I don't know much about him, except that he lives down the street and he's an accountant."

Like Spillman, he didn't have to write it down. He'd remember it. "What's your interest in him?"

I told him about the neighborhood meeting. "See whether there's anything dirty about him, and whether he might have a reason to steal money, as Shirley Durocher was claiming."

"Did she have anything concrete or just suspicions?"

I shrugged. "I don't know anything beyond what she said last night. I'll talk to Alan Prestwick when I get a chance and see what he knows. And while you're at it, check on him, too."

"Will do."

I said bye to Cal, then cleared up the lunch mess and wiped off the table. I threw the cans in the recycling bin and went into the living room where I found the note with Karen Durocher's address. I googled where it was, grabbed my keys, and left.

CHAPTER SEVEN

Karen Durocher lived in a little ranch-style house on the side of a hill in Green Mountain, an older neighborhood on the west side of the city. Most of the homes in Green Mountain were built in the sixties and seventies, some with great views of downtown. Karen's was not one of them. Her yard was small and neglected, dead leaves from a maple tree covering a brown lawn. The house itself was crying out for attention, tan paint peeling, the aluminum windows old and in need of a good wash.

I stepped onto a sagging wood porch and rang the doorbell. I didn't hear anything, but suddenly the door opened. The woman who stood before me looked as worn and ignored as the house.

"Yes?" she said, curiosity in her gravelly voice.

I was struck by how much she looked like Shirley Durocher: the same eyes, the same nose, and even the same dark hair. But this poor woman looked older than her mother.

"Yes?" The tone was now impatient as she smoothed a hand over a wrinkled blouse.

"Are you Karen Durocher?"

"Who wants to know?" she asked.

I introduced myself. "I'm looking into your mother's death."

"Oh?" Her dark eyes surveyed me carefully. "You a cop? I already talked to the cops."

I shook my head.

"You're private," she said.

"That's right."

Her brow wrinkled as she quickly figured things out. "Holly hired you, didn't she?"

"She said you'd say that."

"I'm not dumb."

"I never said you were."

"I thought she'd hire someone because she's on the hot seat."

I stood my ground. "Would you mind if I ask you a few questions? To help Holly."

"Help her?" She snorted again. "I think she's the guilty one."

"That's what I'm trying to figure out."

She stared at me for a long time, thin lips moving in and out as she appeared to argue with herself about what to do. Then she opened the door wider and stepped back.

"Come on in. Don't need the neighbors seeing you and wondering what's going on."

I walked into an open living room that was sparsely decorated, the air stale, the odor of cigarette smoke lingering. Karen went to a threadbare plaid couch and eased onto it, then gestured toward a mismatched blue recliner that had seen better days.

"Have a seat," she said.

The chair faced toward a TV against the opposite wall, so I perched on the edge of the seat to face Karen. She grabbed a pack of cigarettes off a cheap coffee table, lit one, and blew smoke into the air. I glanced toward the kitchen and a few cabinets with broken hinges that needed to be replaced, and the off-white walls all around. I felt the drabness sink into my pores, and I took a deep breath to ward it off. One thing was clear: Karen could've used money.

"You know Holly changed the will," Karen said, smoke coming out of her mouth as she talked.

I tipped my head, not acknowledging that one way or the other. "I don't know that just yet."

She took another drag on the cigarette, then pointed at me with it. "She needs the money."

"How do you know?"

"You think that cupcake shop pays her any money?"

"My understanding is Holly's doing pretty well."

She laughed, a bitter, mean sound. "Yeah, right. She's got big dreams. She wants to open up more shops, and then let them run themselves while she travels. That costs money, more than her little shop will provide."

"How do you know what her shop will provide?"

"She tells me how good business is."

I raised my eyebrows. "You sure about that?"

Her beady little eyes narrowed. "Holly tells me."

I wasn't so sure about that, but I didn't say so. I switched subjects. "If Holly wasn't the original beneficiary, who was?"

She stared at me as if I were stupid. I just wanted to see her reaction when I asked the question.

"Well, me, moron. Who else?"

Name-calling. That was interesting. But I'd been called worse, and it didn't bother me.

I shrugged. "I know nothing about you or your family, so I wondered if someone else would've been in the will."

She shook her head. "I was supposed to inherit my mother's money."

"How do you know that?"

"I just do."

I didn't say anything to that, but let my gaze wander around the room. "You could use the money."

It was a low blow, but I wanted to see what she'd do.

"I don't deny it," she said. "But that doesn't mean I did anything to my mother."

"I didn't say you did."

She stared at me, then put the cigarette in the ashtray and crossed her arms. "You know Holly's got a drug problem."

"I hadn't heard that."

"Oh yeah. She doesn't have a dime to her name, so she changed the will."

"You think Holly created a fake will? The lawyers likely would've caught that."

She waved a hand dismissively. "I'm not saying that. Holly could've coerced Mother into making her the beneficiary."

"How?"

"I don't know. You're the detective, you figure it out." The beady eyes bore into me. "She probably badgered Mother until she finally gave in and changed it."

"I'll look into that, but the will was dated a long time ago."

She shook her head. "That could've been faked to fool me."

I wasn't buying it, but I said, "I'll check it out."

"You do that." She was belligerent, but it was obvious she wanted me to hear her side of things. She picked up her cigarette again, but didn't smoke it. "Holly owes people. You know, off-the-books kind of people. Did you know that?"

"Like bookies?"

"A loan shark, that kind of thing."

Based on the research Cal had done on Holly, and my general impression of her, I doubted that, but I'd check into it all, just to be sure.

"Holly's never been married?"

"No. There might've been a man or two, but I doubt it. She's too shy, and she never got out much. She's smart, but it was all about baking and recipes." She shook her head in disgust. "She could've been a doctor or a lawyer."

"Maybe enjoying what she does is more important. I'd thought I'd be a lawyer, or in finance, but neither career seemed like it would be enjoyable to me," I said. "I always wanted to be a private investigator, so I took a chance, and it worked out."

"Following her dreams was a waste, if you ask me. But it's all about the cupcakes for her."

"What about you?" I asked.

"I've done all right. I was married for a brief time, thought that might last, but it didn't."

I stared at her askance. "Really?" She was a bad liar.

"Why? You don't believe me?"

"I can't find a marriage license."

Those eyes were on me again. "You've been looking into me."

I nodded. "Of course. If you have nothing to hide, it shouldn't be any big deal."

"I don't have anything to hide," she snapped.

"Then why did you tell your daughter that you'd been married when you hadn't? Or am I just having a really hard time digging up the license?"

Her eyes stayed on me for a long time, and then her gaze drifted to the window.

"I just ... never saw the need to marry the guy. But I could tell from the time Holly was little that she wanted to know about her daddy and me. She'd ask all kinds of questions, and I didn't want to disappoint her. So I told her about our wedding, and how beautiful it was, and that then her daddy and I grew apart." She shrugged indifferently. "It's no big deal."

"Okay."

"You're not going to tell her, are you?"

"Not unless I have to," I said. "But Holly was born in 1982. A single mother wasn't that big of a deal."

"I didn't want her to know I wasn't married, all right?"

It felt like there was more to the story, but her stern face told me she wasn't going to say any more. I changed the subject.

"I understand you didn't know your father."

It was pointed, but she took the bait.

"That's right, but what's it to you?"

"I'm curious."

"You're wondering if there's a pattern. My daddy left when I was little, and so did Holly's daddy."

"I don't know what I'm wondering at this point, I'm just asking the question."

"Don't read anything into it. My mother divorced my father when I was little, and that's all there is to it."

I contained my surprise. But why wasn't there a marriage license for Shirley and the mystery husband? I wondered why Cal couldn't find it.

"What was your relationship with your mother like?" I asked.

"My mother? You knew her, right?"

"But I didn't really *know* her."

"She was mean and cranky. I wasn't close to her because she was judgmental, and once I could, I hightailed it out of Texas and came to Denver. I didn't talk to her often, and I didn't let Holly see her much, either. That's why I can't believe that Holly would've wanted to help her out when she did. I don't get it."

I wanted to point out that maybe it was because Karen herself was mean and judgmental, but I bit back the comment.

"Who would want to murder your mother?"

"Besides Holly?"

"That's an awful thing to think of your own daughter."

The lips went in and out. "You don't know her."

"Fair enough." I went on. "Putting Holly aside for a moment, who else might have a motive to murder Shirley?"

"Maybe one of the neighbors?"

"Why do you say that?"

"One of the times I talked to my mother on the phone, I think she was fighting with someone. I could hear her yell something to a man in the background. I asked who it was, and she said one of the neighbors."

"Did she give you a name?"

I wondered if it could've been Mr. Bonifacio. I'd have to ask him about that.

She shook her head. "Mother didn't say, and I didn't ask."

"Where were you the night your mother was murdered?"

She finished her cigarette and crushed it out in an old glass ashtray. "You think I had something to do with her death?"

I didn't respond.

"The police asked me that, too. I was with a friend."

"Who?"

"I'm not telling you that."

"Were you at his house?"

"How do you know it's a he?"

"A guess."

She stared at me, then shook her head, suddenly distrustful. "We were at Buddy's Bar. We were there that night. The bartender would know, too."

"What's the bartender's name?"

"Paul Kava. With a 'K.' " She glared at me. "I told you, the police checked up on me."

"If the police verified your alibi, that's good enough for me."

It wasn't, but I wanted her to let her guard down again.

"I don't have anything to hide."

She sat back and crossed her arms, signaling she'd said what she was going to. I stood up.

"Thanks for your time," I said.

"Yeah, okay."

I held out my business card, but she didn't take it, so I left it on the table. She scowled at me.

"You look into Holly," she said.

I nodded and crossed the room in two strides. She was still on the couch when I let myself out.

As I walked down the sidewalk to my car, I thought about Karen. She was critical and mean, just like her own mother seemed to be, but she couldn't see it. I couldn't help contrasting Karen Durocher to my own mother. I never thought I'd hear myself admit it, but I was lucky. I smiled at the thought. True, my mother can drive me nuts with her worrying and fussing, but she loves me dearly and wants the best for me. And she and my father love Willie, too. There was a lot to be said for that.

I hopped into the 4-Runner and headed down the street.

CHAPTER EIGHT

I drove around the corner and pulled to the curb. Then I got out my phone and dialed a familiar number.

"Reed, dear. How are you?" My mother's high-pitched voice sounded surprised. "I wasn't expecting your call. Is everything all right?"

"I'm fine. Just thought I'd call to say hello."

"Well this is nice. How is everything? Are you and Willie expecting?"

I put a hand to my forehead. My mother used to worry that I was doing drugs, and that I would never get married. Now her fear – besides her worry that I was in constant danger in my job – was that I would never give her grandchildren.

"For now, you'll just have to live with Humphrey."

"Dear, he is a cute kitten, but it's not the same."

"I know."

"Willie did send some photos the other day. That cat is sure silly, isn't he?"

"Yes."

We chatted for a few minutes, and then I asked to speak to my father. He was playing golf, so I told her I'd let her go.

"Reed." She paused. "Are you sure nothing's wrong?"

I glanced in the rearview mirror, thinking of Karen Durocher. "Everything's fine. I love you."

"I love you, too, dear. Thanks for calling."

I ended the call, and could picture my mother on the balcony of her Florida condo right now, pleasantly surprised by her son's behavior. Then I was sure she'd call Willie to make sure I was all right.

I put my phone back in my pocket, then stared out the windshield again and thought about Karen Durocher. I couldn't tell how much of what she was saying was the truth and how much wasn't, but it was clear that she was jealous of her daughter. That didn't sit well with me, but I didn't know if that meant Karen was capable of murdering her mother to keep Holly from getting the inheritance.

Karen had also tried to implicate Mr. Bonifacio. And he'd had a relationship with Shirley. Those things combined meant that I should talk to him. I glanced at the dashboard clock. A few minutes before two. Since Bonifacio lived down the street from me, I'd have time to make some other stops, and then I could talk to him when I went home. I'd told Willie that morning that it'd be nice if we could go to dinner after she got off work, and I hoped with my new case that I'd still be able to do that.

I fished my phone from my pocket again, got on the internet, and looked up Buddy's Bar. It was on Colfax, and there was a phone number listed. I dialed it, waited, and then a high-pitched feminine voice answered.

"Buddy's."

"Is Paul Kava there?" I asked.

"He usually works from noon to close, and he's off on Tuesdays."

"I see," I said.

"Thanks for calling."

"Wait. Is a guy there that comes in with a woman named Karen Durocher? They come in quite a bit."

"What's he look like?"

"I don't know," I said truthfully.

"Sorry, can't help you."

The line went dead.

I put my phone away and thought about my next move. Alan Prestwick was high on my list of people to talk to. Since he was the HOA president, he would have the inside scoop – if there was any – on Phil Epstein's embezzlement. And I wanted to know about Prestwick's altercation with Shirley the night she'd been murdered. That made him look suspicious, but did it mean he'd killed her? My plan in place, I pulled back into the street, got onto Union and then Sixth Avenue, and headed toward downtown.

On the way, I thought about Prestwick. I didn't know a lot about him, except that he'd lived in the neighborhood for several years, in a condo complex the next block over from me. He'd once told me that he and his wife had lived in the suburbs, but once their kids had graduated from college and moved on, they'd wanted to be closer to downtown for the theaters and some of the nicer restaurants and bars. Somewhere I'd heard that he was an engineer and that he worked in a firm at a building on Seventeenth and Curtis. I also heard he was close to retirement. Prestwick might have told me the name of his company, but I couldn't remember it now. Glenway, or Fairway – something with a "way" in it.

I parked on Curtis Street and walked into the building at Seventeenth and Curtis. The lobby was large, with a bank of elevators to the left. I found an electronic directory, swiped the screen to get started, and began looking at the company listings. I wanted to say Prestwick's company started with an "F," like "Freeway." Then I saw it. Fenway Engineering. It was on the fifteenth floor. I strolled to the elevator, got on, and rode up.

The doors opened into a lobby where a woman sat across from the elevator at a large black desk. Apparently Fenway rented the entire floor. The woman was busy at her computer, but she looked up with a pleasant smile when she saw me.

"May I help you?"

"Is Alan Prestwick available?"

She picked up the phone receiver. "Is he expecting you?"

I shook my head.

"Your name?"

"Reed Ferguson."

She punched a button on a console, waited a moment, then murmured into the phone. Then she set the receiver back.

"He'll be right out."

I thanked her and stood to the side for a minute. Once it was clear that Prestwick wasn't coming "right out," I sat down on a black couch and thumbed through an old *Sports Illustrated*. I'm a huge Denver Broncos fan, but this edition was focused on basketball, which I don't watch as much, so the articles meant little to me. Finally I heard a familiar voice.

"Hello, Reed."

I stood up. Alan Prestwick was in brown slacks and a white shirt with the sleeves rolled up. He walked over and held out a hand.

"Hi, Alan," I said.

"This is an unexpected surprise. What can I do for you?"

He did seem surprised, his eyes a little wide, his mouth slightly open.

"Do you have a few minutes to talk about Shirley Durocher?"

He glanced over his shoulder. If the receptionist heard him – or cared – she wasn't showing it.

"Why don't you come back to my office?"

He whirled around, and I followed him down a long hall, past offices and cubicles. He turned into a corner office and waved for me to follow. The office had the usual, desk-and-shelves combo I'd seen in so many offices. He sat down in a tall chair. The windows faced west and north, but instead of a view of the Rocky Mountains, all he could see when he looked out was the silver metal and windows of a building next door and a parking lot. Too bad, because the views from here would've been gorgeous otherwise. I took a chair across from the desk and smiled at him.

"It's such terrible news about Shirley Durocher," he said.

"Yes," I replied. "When did you hear about her?"

"The police talked to me a few days ago." His expression changed as he realized why I might be talking to him. "You're a PI."

I nodded.

"You're looking into her death."

"For her granddaughter," I said. "She wants to find the murderer as much or more than the police." I left out that Holly was a likely suspect in her grandmother's death, and that she wanted her name cleared.

"I see."

I didn't want to confront him immediately with the argument I'd overheard between him and Shirley the night she'd been murdered, so I started with, "How well did you know Shirley?"

He sat back and put his hands on the arms of his chair, trying for casual, but he didn't quite make it.

"Not very well. Mostly from dealing with her at the association meetings. And a time or two I had to go over to her house to discuss something she brought up."

"Oh? What things?"

"The thefts in the neighborhood, and a particularly pesky barking dog."

"What was your impression of her?"

"She seemed nice enough."

"Huh. That's not what others say."

"Is that so?"

"Most people thought she was cranky and mean."

"Maybe they didn't understand her." He held up a hand, then let it drop. "And why speak ill of the dead?"

"What do you know about this accounting issue she was referring to at the last association meeting, and her accusations of Phil Epstein?"

"That's the first I heard of anything, and it caught me off-guard, to tell you the truth. I talked to Phil afterward, and he said he had no idea what she was talking about."

"But you're looking into it?"

"Of course," he said.

"You wouldn't mind letting me know what you find out, would you? Not just for my investigation of her death, but as an association member, we all need to know if there is anything fishy going on with our money."

"Yes, I'll be letting everyone know if there's an issue."

"Have you had any other problems with Epstein? Has he acted suspicious about anything?"

"No, nothing like that. He's been a little stressed because he recently went through a nasty divorce, but I don't see how that's any of your business."

I arched an eyebrow.

He cleared his throat. "Like I said, I was surprised by what Shirley said."

"How long has Epstein been the association bookkeeper?"

"A little over two years."

"And no problems with him? No one else has accused him of any wrongdoing?"

"Not at all. I vetted him carefully and checked his resume. Everything is fine."

His answers were smooth, but he seemed slightly nervous. Was talking to a PI bringing that out, or was there something more?

"Have you had a chance to check the accounting books for the association to make sure everything is as it should be?" I asked.

"Not yet, but I have an appointment with Phil later this week."

"And you talked to the police about Shirley and Epstein's argument at the meeting?" I asked.

"Yes. They knew about the situation with Phil. I don't know who told them that."

I kept a straight face, knowing that I'd shared that information with Spillman.

"I told them everything I knew," he went on.

I sat a little straighter. "Which is what you told me."

"Yes."

"Did you tell them about the argument you'd had with Shirley after the meeting?"

His jaw dropped. "What argument?"

"You and Shirley were talking around the side of the building."

He turned white. "I don't—"

I held up a hand. "You can't get out of this." I recounted the conversation I'd heard. "It sounded like she threatened you." I slowly lifted a finger and pointed at him. "And you threatened her."

He gulped. "It wasn't like that."

"How'd you explain the argument to the police?"

"We were arguing about Phil, that's all. She said she knew more about the situation and she'd share it here at work if I didn't do something about him."

"Why would anyone here care?"

He shrugged. "She thought she could ruin my reputation, I guess."

I stared at him. It was a lame lie.

"You're sure about that?" I finally asked.

"Yes. That's all there is to it." He was sticking to it.

"You sounded a bit hostile to her."

He scoffed at that. "I'd had a long day, and I was a little uptight, but it was nothing I would act on."

"What did you do the rest of the evening?"

His eyes narrowed. He knew I was asking about his alibi, just as Karen Durocher had known when I asked her the same question.

"I went home."

"To your wife?"

"Yes. She was at the meeting, and afterward we went straight home, watched a little television, and then we went to bed."

I couldn't recall seeing his wife there, but I'd check with Willie and Bob to see if either of them remembered. I wasn't sure if that would be important, but it was easy to follow up on.

"Did the police verify your alibi with your wife?"

He nodded. "Yes. They talked to her a few nights ago." He glanced at his phone. "I really should get back to work. If you have any more questions, could we talk later?"

"Sure." I stood up. "I appreciate your taking time out of your busy day."

"Not at all."

He waved a dismissive hand. I started for the door, then turned around.

"How well did you know Shirley's daughter and grand-daughter?"

He sucked in a breath, disappointed I hadn't left.

"I've never met either one of them," he said. "I've only been to Shirley's house a time or two, and I wasn't there for long."

"How well do you know Mr. Bonifacio?"

"Who?"

"Shirley's neighbor."

He shook his head. "Never heard of him."

"Okay, thanks." I pulled out a business card, crossed back to his desk, and handed it to him. "In case you need to call."

"Sure thing." He took it as if it were a snake, and quickly set it down on the desk.

"If you find out anything more about Phil Epstein, let me know."

"Of course."

"Where does he work?"

He let out a put-upon sigh. "At Doyle-Anderson Accounting."

I went back to the door and let myself into the hall. When I glanced back, he looked relieved to see me go.

CHAPTER NINE

I rode down to the lobby, then googled Doyle-Anderson Accounting. The address was on Colorado Boulevard, not too far from downtown. I glanced at my watch. Almost three. Plenty of time to talk to Phil Epstein before he left work. A few white clouds hung low in the sky as I walked to my 4-Runner and drove east on Seventeenth Avenue to Colorado Boulevard. On the way, I called Bob Smith.

"Hey, Reed." He sounded a lot like Ace and Deuce. "What's up?"

"Have you ever met Alan Prestwick's wife?"

"The HOA president? No, I don't recall ever meeting her. Why?"

"I was just wondering if she'd been at the meeting the other night."

"I'm afraid I can't help you."

"No problem." I thanked him and ended the call. Maybe Willie would know if Prestwick's wife was at the meeting.

I turned south on Colorado and soon saw the Wells Fargo building. It was taller than most in the area, and it was easy to spot with its green-glass windows that reflected the sun. I pulled into the parking lot, went inside, and used a directory to find Doyle-Anderson Accountants. It was on the third floor, so I rode the elevator up, got out, and found it at the end of a long hallway. I pushed through a heavy wooden door and went inside. No one occupied the chair behind a short counter by the door.

I looked around for a bell or buzzer, then called out, "Hello?"

No answer.

I waited a moment, then boldly started down a hallway across from the entrance. In a few offices people were at work at computers. A woman glanced up at me as I passed, but I acted as if I had every reason to be there, and she left me alone. Two doors down, I saw a nameplate by a door. "Phil Epstein." The door was partially open and I peeked inside.

Epstein was sitting at a small desk, gazing at a monitor, his brow wrinkled in concentration. Then he began typing. I took that opportunity to come through the door. He looked up, and his eyes widened in surprise.

"Hey, Phil," I said pleasantly.

"You can't be here."

"I was in the neighborhood," I said, ignoring him, "and I thought I'd stop by to ask you a few questions." I gestured at the chair. "You don't mind, do you?"

He looked over my shoulder and opened his mouth.

"I wouldn't call for help," I said in a low voice. "Then someone might know about the scuttlebutt surrounding you and Shirley."

His jaw clamped shut. I figured that was because of me knowing about him and Shirley, not my use of the word "scut-tlebutt."

He gulped once and said, "Close the door."

I did, then sat down in an uncomfortable chair across from his desk. He drummed the desk with his fingers as he contemplated me.

"What do you want?" he finally asked.

"I want to ask you a few questions about Shirley Durocher, and then I'll leave."

"Fine." His tone was clipped. "Why are you interested in her? Oh, wait, you're a detective. Who hired you?"

I didn't know if he'd ever met Holly, but I wasn't going to tell him that she'd hired me.

"That's confidential," I said. "But I am looking into Shirley's death."

"I know what you're thinking. Because Shirley accused me at that meeting of stealing from the association funds, that must mean I murdered her. Well, I didn't."

"I didn't say that. I just want to find out your side of the story."

"She didn't have a right to accuse me of anything," he said. "I've done nothing wrong."

I nodded. "But why would she say something like that? What about her suspicions?"

"I don't know. I'm not a thief. You can ask anyone here at work. I've done a great job, and I haven't stolen a dime from anyone."

"I'm sure your work record is admirable, but people here wouldn't necessarily know anything about what you do with the association funds."

His jaw was tight, and he didn't reply.

"If Shirley's accusations were unfounded, then why did she say what she did?" I asked.

"Because she's a mean old woman. You get on her bad side, and she's got it in for you."

"How did you get on her bad side?"

"She was at every meeting since I became the bookkeeper for the HOA, and she always had some suggestion or thing that I should be doing with the association funds. She's relentless about telling me how to do my job. A while back I told her to back off, that I knew what I was doing. She didn't take kindly to that."

I didn't attend very many meetings, so I didn't know about their interactions.

"Did anyone else hear you tell her off?"

He shook his head. "Not that I know of. It was after a meeting, and we were alone."

I made a mental note to follow up with Alan Prestwick and ask him if he recalled seeing Shirley heckle Epstein.

"Do you like being the bookkeeper for the association?" I asked.

He shrugged. "It's all right. I know accounting, so it's no big deal."

"How long have you been on the board?"

"Two years now. No one else seems to want to take over for me."

I switched gears. "I understand you went through a nasty divorce a while back."

His eyebrows went up slightly. "So?"

"I also heard that money's tight, that your wife took you to the cleaners."

He glared at me. "Who told you that?"

"It doesn't matter. Is it true?"

He studied me, then finally sighed. "I guess it doesn't hurt to tell you, and if it'll get you out of here that much faster, then fine. You're right, my wife got a good deal in our divorce. She's getting a big alimony check every month, and I pay a lot in child support for my two kids. Plus, we'd racked up a lot of debt during our marriage, so I'm paying off a big portion of that. It stinks. And along with that, I got the condo, but the payments are almost killing me." He said all that fast, and he took in a deep breath. "Are you happy now?"

"I'm not unhappy," I said.

His lips twisted up at the distaste in my humor, and then I could see him put reasoning behind my question.

"You think because I have financial trouble, that must mean I'm stealing association funds like Shirley was saying."

"That's logical, isn't it?"

He glanced away. "I could strangle that old woman," he muttered. Then he turned red.

"For what? Accusing you of what's true?"

"It's not!" he snapped. "I had nothing to do with her murder." He threw up his hands. "This is unbelievable that I'm a suspect just because of what she said at the meeting. I can show you the books. I can account for every penny that the association has, and everything that's been spent."

"I'm sure you can, and you can show Alan all that. I'm also sure you can figure out a way – if you're stealing – of making your accounting appear correct."

He paled. "You're not going to let this go, are you?"

"Not until I find Shirley's killer. So, can I see the books?"

"I don't have the paperwork here. You can stop by tonight. I'll be home by six, and I'll show them to you then."

He stared at me, and I left an uncomfortable silence sit between us. Actually, I was at ease playing this game. He began to sweat, but he was trying hard to act cool.

"I'll be home all evening," he finally said.

"How well did you know Shirley?" I asked.

He was taken aback by my abrupt change of topic. "I only talked to her at the meetings."

"You never went to her house?"

"No way. Why would I go over there? She was a mean lady."

I switched subjects again to keep him on his toes. "How long have you worked here?"

"Over ten years. It's a good job." Then he pointed at me. "You better not ask questions around here, okay? I've got a good reputation, and I don't want you ruining that."

"Okay," I said noncommittally. "Where were you the night Shirley was killed?"

"The night of the HOA meeting."

I nodded.

"I left right away and went home alone," he said. "And before you go poking around my building, no one saw me. The police have already been asking questions, and I don't need you there, too. I know it makes me look bad, that I don't have an alibi, but that's the way it is. I didn't have anything to do with Shirley's death, you got that?"

"I got it."

"What do you know about the burglaries in the neighborhood?"

He looked away and shrugged. "Beats me. I think it's either some kids, or maybe some homeless people."

"Have you had anything stolen?"

He shook his head. "You?"

I smiled. "No. Maybe the thieves know better than to steal from a private investigator."

I thought that might draw a laugh from him, but he just glared at me. Then he stood up. "You need to go now."

He stared down at me, trying to intimidate me, but after years on the job, I don't scare easily. I waited until he was good and uncomfortable again, then I stood up.

He went to the door. "And don't come here again." He opened the door and waited, his eyes blazing.

I stepped into the doorway, and even though Epstein was furious, he quietly closed the door so as not to draw attention to himself or me. I walked down the hallway and into the reception area. It was still empty. I walked out to the elevators, thinking about Epstein.

He was angry and rattled. And there was more than he was telling me, but I wasn't sure what.

CHAPTER TEN

I sat in my car and put in a CD of The Psychedelic Furs, one of my favorite '80s bands, and thought about my conversation with Epstein. He hadn't been happy to see me. I could attribute some of his nervousness to my unexpected arrival, but there seemed to be more than that. But whether it had something to do with Shirley's accusing him of cooking the HOA books, or with her murder, I didn't know. I shook my head, trying to clear my thoughts. I'd been at this case all day, and I wasn't any closer to knowing who might've wanted to murder Shirley.

After a minute, I turned down the music, pulled out my phone, and dialed Detective Spillman, thinking she might be able to give me a little more information. I didn't expect a lot, since Shirley's murder was an active investigation, but anything Spillman might tell me could be helpful. After four rings, the call went to voice mail, so I asked her to call me and put my phone back in my pocket.

It was warm, and I rolled down my window. I was just about to call Cal when Phil Epstein came through the glass doors of the Wells Fargo building. His face was pinched in consternation as he talked on his cell phone. He glanced my way, and I ducked down, then peered over the dashboard. He was hurrying the other direction, across the parking lot. He stopped at a beat-up Mazda and got in. A moment later, the car careened through the parking lot, and he screeched to a halt at Colorado. He waited for a break in traffic, then turned north. I started the 4-Runner and followed.

It was now almost four, and rush-hour traffic was building. The Psychedelic Furs were singing "Love My Way." I cranked up the volume again and listened while I drove slowly up Colorado Boulevard. I kept several cars between Epstein's Mazda and my car, and I doubted he had any idea I was tailing him.

Epstein continued north. He seemed to be in a hurry because he was switching lanes and darting around cars, but with the heavy volume of traffic, it was difficult. I kept him in sight, except for a moment I thought I'd lost him when he sped through a stoplight at Sixth Avenue, and I didn't. But once I made it through the next green light, I spotted the Mazda in the left lane. He drove up to Twenty-sixth Avenue and turned left. Traffic was lighter, but there were still plenty of cars between us.

The Mazda went west to Emerson Street, then south one block, where it pulled over halfway down the street. We were in Five Points, one of Denver's oldest neighborhoods. When I was growing up, it had not been a good part of town, but it had recently gone through a gentrification and was now a mix of updated houses and older apartments. Epstein had parked in front of a four-story apartment building that clearly hadn't been a part of the new construction that surrounded it.

I stopped at the corner and watched as Epstein got out and walked across the lawn, and up the outside stairs to the third floor of the apartment building. He went down the walkway and stopped at a door, then knocked. It opened seconds later, and he went inside. I couldn't see who had answered the door. I waited and watched the apartment, then pulled out my phone and called Cal.

"What's up?" he barked into the phone.

No "O Great Detective." That meant he was busy.

"I'm watching Phil Epstein," I said. "He just went into an apartment near Twenty-sixth and Emerson."

"Not the greatest neighborhood."

"Eh, it's still spotty."

"What's he doing there?"

"Beats me. Have you found out any more on him?"

I waited for him to say he was busy with work, but instead he said, "I've done a bit of research, in between some things I'm doing for my client. His ex-wife is Laura, and she's an adjunct professor at Metro."

Metropolitan State University is located just west of downtown, and it is one of the state's more affordable universities. I sometimes go to the campus because the Tivoli Brewing Company is located there, and I like some of their beers.

"Not bad," I said as I watched the apartment building. A few people came and went, but not Epstein.

"She does all right, salary-wise," he went on.

"He went through a bad divorce. Have you been able to look at his finances?"

"Uh-huh. He's paying a hefty chunk of change in alimony and child support each month."

"What does that leave him?"

"His mortgage payment is pretty high, and it looks like he had a Mercedes that he recently paid off."

"He's driving a junker now," I said. "Maybe his ex has the Mercedes."

"Could be, but the car's in his name. He hardly has any

money in his checking and savings accounts, and it looks like he had to split his 401k with her. So if he said she took him for a lot of money, he's right. It appears he's had some medical expenses, too, and he's racking up some credit card debt."

"So money's tight," I said.

"You can say that again."

I was tempted to, but didn't. "Is his job supporting him?"

"Just barely."

"Any issues with his work?"

"No. He's been at that company for ten years, regularly gets raises and bonuses. If it wasn't for the divorce, he'd be in good shape."

"No trouble in his past?"

"Nothing. Not even a parking ticket."

I thought for a second. "Do me a favor. See if you can find anything on the association, a checking account, that kind of thing."

"Do you have a bank name?"

"No." I told him the association name. "Would that help? And if not, I can get the bank information. It should be available to the homeowners."

"That would be helpful," he said with a hint of sarcasm.

I ignored that. "Did you check on Alan Prestwick?"

"I haven't, but I will. You need anything right away?"

"No. I already talked to him, but I'd like to see if what you find matches what he told me."

"You think he had something to do with Shirley's death?"

"Hmm," I said. "I don't know. I think there was more to his argument with her than he's saying, but I don't know if that means he murdered her. So far, no one I've talked to is sticking out as a clear suspect. But I can't eliminate anyone, either."

"We've got to find that person, to help Holly."

"You really like her, don't you?"

"I'm just trying to be helpful," he said innocently.

Just then, Epstein came out of the apartment and strolled down the walkway to the stairs.

"I have to let you go," I said. "My suspect is heading back to his car."

"I'll call you later." With that, he was gone.

I pocketed my phone and scrunched down in my seat as Epstein reached the ground floor and headed across the lawn to his car. He got in and drove away. I let him get to the corner, then I started down the block. He stayed on Emerson, and I tailed him to Twentieth, where he turned west. I had a pretty good idea he was heading home. Sure enough, a few minutes later, he turned down Sherman Street and then into the underground parking garage of his building. I continued down the street, went around the block, and drove back to the apartment building on Emerson Street that he'd visited earlier.

A few cars went by as I watched the building for a minute. I figured out the unit number for the apartment Epstein had visited, then got out and crossed the lawn to an open breezeway that had a bank of locked mailboxes. I looked up the unit number for the apartment Epstein had gone into. The nameplate read "McKane." It meant nothing to me.

I went back to the 4-Runner and watched the apartment for a while. I was curious about McKane, if that's who Epstein had visited. Did his sudden visit here have anything to do with my questioning him? I had no way of knowing. I also had no way to know whether Epstein and McKane were involved in Shirley's murder. McKane might just be Epstein's friend or someone he owed money to.

These thoughts were occupying my mind when a dark-haired man with a ponytail emerged from McKane's apartment. He strolled down the stairs and to a parking lot on the north side of the building. A moment later, an old black Camaro pulled onto the street, and he was at the wheel. For the third time that day, I tailed someone.

The Camaro went north to Twenty-sixth, then east. We crossed Colorado Boulevard and ended up on Quebec Street, in the Stapleton neighborhood. The old Stapleton airport had once been here, but after Denver International Airport had been built several miles northeast, this area was turned into an urban neighborhood of shops and housing. The Camaro crossed Quebec and parked in a lot with several shops and restaurants. I pulled into a space a safe distance away from the Camaro and watched. Ponytail got out and went into a jewelry store.

I grabbed my binoculars, which I store in the seat behind me, and trained them on the storefront. Through the glass, I saw Ponytail talking to a man behind the counter. Then Pony-tail pulled something – a piece of jewelry, I assumed – from his pocket and handed it to the man, who picked up his magnifying loupe and held it against one eye as he studied the piece. He finally set down the eyepiece and handed the jewelry back to Ponytail. They talked for a minute, then Ponytail came back outside. But instead of going to his car, he turned and went two doors down to the Smashburger. I waited and watched with the binoculars, and I soon saw him with a tray of food. He sat near the window and bit into his burger. My stomach growled.

"I think it's time to go home," I said to no one as I put the binoculars away.

I didn't think there was any more I could do now, and I was wondering if I'd gone on a wild-goose chase. I had no idea if Ponytail's little trip to the jeweler had anything to do with Phil Epstein. I called Willie as I got onto Quebec.

"Hey, babe," she said.

"How're you?"

"Not bad. Work was hectic. What're you up to?"

"On a case." I told her what had happened since Cal had

THE DAMNED DON'T DIE

showed up at lunchtime, and ended with, "I'm headed home now."

"Good. I don't feel like going out. Is that okay with you?"

"Sure."

"I'll start dinner, and you can catch me up when you get here."

"Sounds great."

I thought I'd enjoy the rest of the evening with Willie, but it didn't turn out that way.

CHAPTER ELEVEN

I parked on the street in front of my building, headed up the sidewalk, and stepped onto the porch. As I started toward the side of the building, a voice startled me, and I jumped in a very un-Bogie-like fashion.

"Everybody's saying I did it, but I didn't."

I whirled around, my heart beating a staccato rhythm in my chest. I peered into the shadows behind me. Mr. Bonifacio stepped slowly onto the porch.

"Did what?" I asked.

"The neighbors are saying I killed Shirley."

He held his right hand down by his side, and something was in his hand. With the growing gloom, I couldn't tell what it was. A gun? Then he raised his hand, and I saw that he had a butcher knife.

Not a gun, but certainly a weapon. I took a subtle step back and pointed at him.

"What's with the knife?"

"Huh? Oh." He waved it around. "I was getting dinner ready when I looked up and saw you out the window, so I came over to talk to you." His hand dropped back to his side. "Why would people say I killed her?"

"You were involved with her."

"That doesn't mean I would hurt her, let alone ... kill her."

"And you kept your relationship with her a secret," I said. "Some people might think the two of you had something to hide."

"We knew how people could talk and fuss about it. Two older people getting together. You know what they'd say."

I shrugged. "I don't know that anyone would've cared."

He suddenly took a step forward. I watched his knife hand, but he kept it at his side. "Wait a minute. Who's saying I was seeing Shirley?"

"The police."

He squinted through his thick glasses. "Oh, you're the detective, so you're looking into her murder, huh?"

It seemed everyone was coming to that conclusion about me.

"Who hired you?" he asked.

"That's confidential."

"Oh, I bet it was her granddaughter, Holly."

"You know her?"

"I've seen her around a time or two, and Shirley talked about her."

"What does she look like?"

"She's got long brown hair, and she's quiet."

I nodded, but didn't confirm that Holly had hired me. But he knew.

"Let's get back to why you think people suspect you're the murderer."

"Well, I ..." He blustered.

"Shirley's daughter said that you and Shirley had been fighting about something."

"That's not true."

"Were you with Shirley the night she was murdered?"

"Yes. I stopped by after the meeting and we had a drink. But I left right after that."

Interesting. If Bonifacio had told Spillman that, she hadn't shared it with me.

"Did anyone see you at her house, or see you go home?" I asked.

His jaw dropped.

"No one did," I said.

He shook his head. "Not that I know of."

"Have you talked to the police about this?"

"Yes." His eyes darted around. He had a problem if he couldn't prove that he'd left Shirley's house when he said he had. "Wait. I saw someone else hanging around her house when I left."

"Who?"

"I don't know."

I stared at him. "Unless you can find that person, it's easy to assume you were there longer than you say."

"I wasn't," he said harshly.

"What did this person look like?"

"He was kind of tall, and he had on dark clothes."

"You're sure it was a guy?"

"I think so."

"Was he wearing a hat, or a hoodie?"

"A hoodie?"

"A sweatshirt with a hood."

"I don't remember."

I contemplated him with a wry smile. "I'm not sure any of this information helps you."

"Maybe not, but it's the truth."

Or are you lying, trying to get me to look elsewhere, I thought.

Maybe since he didn't see or hear too well, he didn't really have any idea who he saw.

"What did you do when you left Shirley's house?" I asked.

"I went home and watched a little TV, and then I went to bed."

"Alone?"

"Of course. I'm not seeing anyone but Shirley."

"So you don't have an alibi."

His wrinkled face went white.

I moved on. "Have you had any problems with thieves around your house? Anything stolen?"

"No, and I've got a gun in the house, so they better watch out."

Good Lord, I thought. The man could barely see or hear. I shuddered to think who might get hurt, him or the thieves. Or anyone else at the wrong place.

"Did Shirley talk about things being stolen?" I went on.

He nodded. "I don't know if she had anything swiped, but she was worried that someone was watching her house."

"She mentioned that at the meeting."

"Yes. She was concerned that thieves were casing her house."

"Along with people not cleaning up their leaves," I said drily.

He shrugged. "It can be a problem."

There was a question I was dying to ask him, but I didn't quite know how to bring it up.

"With Shirley ... um ..." I was dancing around the issue, and I finally said, "What was it about her? Why did you like her, because no one else seemed to?"

He tipped his head to the side. "I know people say she was mean, and she could be abrupt. But there was a different side to her that most people didn't see. She could be fun, and she was passionate. Honestly, she was dynamite in the sack. My Viagra—"

"Stop!" I put my hands over my ears. "I don't want to know the details."

He smiled. "You asked."

"Yeah, but I – never mind."

"I didn't start out with the intent to *date* her. One day I helped her bring in some groceries, and she showed me her collection of pottery. After that, she had me over for dinner, and one thing led to another. Then I spent the night."

"Okay," I cut him off. "Did Shirley ever talk about having enemies?"

"She didn't like her ex."

"Did she have contact with him?"

"I don't know. I just know that when she mentioned her marriage, it wasn't fondly, if you know what I mean. There were no kind words for him. I think he might've hit her. She never trusted him."

"Is this guy still around?"

He pursed his lips. "He might be. There was one evening she took a phone call, and she was arguing with some fellow. I asked about him, and she told me he was into some shady stuff, but that's all she would say."

"You told the police all this?"

"Of course. I don't want them thinking I did anything to Shirley. If anything—" He choked up and cleared his throat. "I cared about her a lot."

"I see," I murmured. He seemed genuinely distraught.

"You ask me," he said, "the police should be looking at Phil Epstein."

"Why?"

"Like Shirley said, he was stealing from the HOA, and

wouldn't he come after her for accusing him in public like she did?"

"Did she have proof that he was stealing?"

"I don't know, but you heard her at the meeting."

I nodded and decided not to argue with him about whether Shirley's accusation constituted proof.

My phone beeped, and I glanced at the screen. Willie had texted, wondering where I was.

"I'm sorry you feel like everyone thinks you did something to Shirley," I said, "but I'm on the case, if that makes you feel any better."

He looked me up and down. "I don't know. Are you a good detective?"

"I can hold my own."

"All right. You find her killer."

He spun around, the knife still at his side. I waited until I saw him disappear into his house, then I headed up the stairs. I was shaking my head when I came into the condo. Humphrey bounded up and started playing around my ankles. I picked him up and scratched behind his ears.

"How're you, little guy?" I said.

He started purring. Willie was in the kitchen, so I went into there.

"Hey, hon." I gave her a kiss.

Humphrey meowed, and she gave *him* a kiss.

"He's something else," she said. "He's got all kinds of energy." Then she looked at me. "What took you so long?"

"I was downstairs talking to Mr. Bonifacio."

"Oh?" She was just putting meatloaf into the oven.

I set Humphrey down. "You want something to drink?"

"I'd love a glass of wine."

I got out a bottle and glasses, and while she washed her hands, I poured us drinks. Then we sat down at the table, and I filled her in on my day, including what Mr. Bonifacio had told me.

"I have a hard time picturing Shirley and Mr. Bonifacio together," I said when I finished. "But I have a hard time picturing Shirley with anybody."

"She was not the kindest woman," she said as Humphrey jumped up on her lap and went to sleep. "But maybe they were both vulnerable. He's recently lost his wife, and maybe she was lonely. And one thing led to another."

I held up a hand. "Stop! Mr. Bonifacio already told me about how his Viagra was helping him."

She burst out laughing. "You didn't tell me that."

"Uh-huh."

I got up and pulled salad stuff out of the fridge. I prepared a salad as we talked.

"You've had a busy day," she said. "Any idea who murdered her?"

"Not a clue. Oh, do you know if Alan Prestwick's wife was at the HOA meeting?"

She pursed her lips. "I think so. Why?"

"Just following up on what Prestwick said." And he was telling the truth. "Oh, and you're never going to believe this."

She glanced at me. "What?"

"Cal seems to be interested in Holly."

"You're kidding."

I grinned. "Nope."

"I wondered if a woman would ever catch his eye. Let me guess, he was too terrified to talk to her."

"On the contrary. He kept jumping into the conversation, and he volunteered my services. I've never seen him so bold. But I don't know if he'll be able to ask her out. Even if he has the opportunity, I doubt he'll take it."

"You'll have to help him along. Help him with what to say."

I nodded. Willie had an amused look on her face as we chatted while I got the rest of dinner ready and ate.

"Do you have to work tonight?" she asked as we cleared the dishes.

"I need to talk to Phil Epstein and get the HOA accounting records, but that's all."

"How about a movie when you get back?"

"Sure. Want to watch *The Damned Don't Cry*?"

"Instead of film noir tonight, how about a rom-com?"

I pretended to be offended that she didn't want to watch my choice, but then smiled. "That'll be fine."

She flicked a dish towel at me. I caught the end of it, pulled her close, and kissed her.

"Maybe we can forget about the movie."

"Maybe," she said, then stepped back. "Go run your errand and hurry back."

"I will."

I headed out the door, fully intending to be back as soon as I could.

CHAPTER TWELVE

I went downstairs, and as I rounded the corner to the front porch, I ran into the Goofballs.

"Hey, Reed," Ace said in his slow drawl.

I smiled. "Hey, how are you two?"

"Just fine." Deuce jerked his thumb toward the other side of the building, where his truck was parked. "We're going to B 52s. Wanna come along?"

I shook my head. "No, guys. I've got an errand to run, and then I told Willie I'd watch a movie."

"A film noir?" Deuce pronounced it very carefully.

"No," I said. "Probably a rom-com."

Ace stared at me. "A what?"

"A romantic comedy."

"Oh," they said in unison.

"I think the film no-are would be better," Deuce whispered to Ace.

I smiled and started to step past them.

"How's your case?" Ace asked.

"It's early," I said. "I've only been at it today, but it feels like a lot longer."

"What's up?" Deuce was all ears. He fancies himself a detective, and my assistant. Specifically, he always fantasized about getting to carry a gun. Not on my watch, that's for sure.

Ace turned to him. "I forgot to tell you. He's helping Holly Durocher because the police think she might've killed her grandmother."

"Holly wouldn't do that to Shirley," Deuce said. Then he looked at me. "You need any help?"

"Yeah," Ace nodded. "Holly's really nice, and we can help her out."

His crush on Holly hadn't gone away.

"Now that you mention it," I said. "There is something you two could do."

Deuce held up a hand. "As long as it isn't watching a house. That's so boring."

They always want to help, but they hate surveillance, and they never fail to let me know that. It narrows my options for what I can ask them to do.

"Nothing like that," I went on. "I think you'll like this better."

"Oh yeah?" they said together. Their eyes were wide in anticipation.

"Do you guys have some time on your hands tomorrow?"

"I have to work, but not until tomorrow afternoon," Ace said.

"I'm available after work," Deuce chimed in.

"Perfect," I said. "Anytime will work. I want you two to talk to Shirley's neighbors. Find out if anyone heard or saw anything the night she was murdered. Ask if they saw anyone visit Shirley, or leave her house. And ask if they ever heard her arguing with anyone. Stuff like that."

"You want us to start with Mr. and Mrs. Darmody?" Ace asked.

I nodded. "That would be good."

"We can do that right now," Deuce said.

"Yep." Ace smiled. "We can play pool anytime."

I laughed. "If that's what you want to do."

They nodded enthusiastically.

"Give me a call if you hear anything interesting or unusual," I said.

Ace started down the porch steps. "This'll be great."

"Right." Deuce was right behind him.

They chatted as they walked down the sidewalk. I watched them for a moment, then headed in the other direction, toward Phil Epstein's four-story condo building, which had been renovated a few years back. From what I'd heard, the units cost a pretty penny.

I entered the foyer, which had a glass security door and a bank of mailboxes. There was a panel with buzzers, and I found one for Epstein. I pressed the button and waited. He didn't answer, so I pressed the button again and held my finger on it. That should get his attention.

"Come on, Phil," I muttered. "I haven't got all night."

I glanced at my watch. It was almost seven. He'd said he'd be in all evening, but apparently he'd blown me off. Or he was ignoring me. I pursed my lips. If he knew me, he would realize I don't give up that easily. I pressed the button one final time, then peered through the glass and down a hallway.

Empty.

Since there was no one around to open the door, I waited, ready to use the oldest trick in the book. A few minutes later, a man in a suit walked up the sidewalk and came in through the front door. He didn't even look at me as he crossed the foyer and used a key to unlock the security door. He went inside, and

I quietly grabbed the door before it closed. The man didn't even glance back as I went through and headed for the stairs. So much for security.

I took the stairs up to the third floor and walked down the hall to Epstein's condo. I knocked on the door and it moved. I hadn't noticed it was cracked open. I pushed on the door, and it opened a little wider. I glanced inside. The condo was dark. I rapped on the door again and called out.

"Phil?"

Nothing.

I looked around. The hall was empty.

I should leave this alone, I thought. But I couldn't resist.

I darted into the condo and quietly shut the door behind me. Then I felt around on the wall for a switch and turned on the lights, wondering for a moment what I'd find. Epstein's body lying on the floor? But nothing so dramatic greeted me when the light illuminated the room.

The floor plan was open, with a living area directly in front of me, and a kitchen-dining area to the right. The opposite wall was mostly windows covered with closed blinds. I tiptoed across a hardwood floor and into the room. Then I looked on the other side of a couch that faced a TV hung on the wall. I had a vision of Epstein lying wounded near the couch, but thankfully that wasn't the case. I sneaked into the kitchen, which was nicely done in cherry cabinets and stainless steel appliances, but he wasn't there, either. I hurried back across the main room and down a short hall, where I quickly checked a bathroom and then the master suite. Epstein was nowhere to be found.

Assured that I was alone, I went back into the kitchen and inspected it more closely. The cabinets were tidy, holding some canned goods, spaghetti and sauce, and Hamburger Helper. The refrigerator was almost empty. Indicative of a man who didn't have a lot of money to spend.

I went back into the main room. A few magazines, an iPhone, a few iPods, and two tablets were sitting on a coffee table. I picked up the phone and swiped the screen, but it was off. I powered it up, but it was password-protected, so I turned it back off. I ran into the same thing with the tablets.

Why the extras? I wondered. Maybe for his kids?

Some CDs and DVDs were neatly organized in a cabinet next to the TV, but other than that, the room was bare. I picked up some mail that was sitting on the arm of the couch. It had all been opened, so I peered inside the envelopes. There were some bills, and one was a notice from a collection agency. One envelope had a return address from Laura Epstein. His wife? I looked inside the envelope, but it was empty.

I was engrossed in the mail and didn't hear the noise until it was near Epstein's door. I set the envelopes down and tiptoed to the door, then peered through the peephole. A woman was standing at a door directly across the hall. She pulled keys from her purse, and as she unlocked her door, she glanced over at Epstein's door. I moved to the side of the peephole and held my breath. Was she observant enough to see the sudden light at the peephole?

I put my ear to the door and listened. Then I heard her door open. I looked through the peephole again. The woman had her door ajar, but she was still looking at Epstein's door. Then she stepped inside her place and the door slammed shut. I let out my breath and waited a moment to see if she'd emerge. When she didn't, I turned and hurried down the hall to the condo's bathroom.

It didn't take me long to inspect it, as there was little in it except for extra toilet paper in the cabinet under the sink. I went into the master suite. It was sparsely furnished and lacked any sense of hominess. If Epstein was dating anyone, I saw no signs of it.

I checked in his dresser drawers. Tee shirts in the drawers were slightly ruffled. In one drawer, two small, blue jewelry boxes were lying haphazardly on top of his underwear. I opened the boxes. They were empty. Did they belong to Phil's ex?

I shrugged, then went to the walk-in closet and checked around. Some of the clothes on hangers were a bit askew. Several pairs of shoes were on the floor, but they were not quite as neatly arranged as I would have thought. I rubbed my chin. Something about his clothes bothered me. They were folded or hung up, but it seemed as if someone might have rifled through them.

I moved back to the dresser and stared into a drawer for a minute. Had someone gone through his things, or was I imagining something? Then my eyes fell on two photos, a boy and a girl, that sat on the dresser. They'd been moved because I could see where the dust had been. Had someone picked them up recently? I shrugged. Someone, like Epstein.

The final thing to check was a small desk in the corner. The drawers held spare paper and pens and other office supplies. I looked for a ledger or anything that might've been from the HOA, but didn't find anything. A power cord ran from the wall outlet and lay on the desk, but there was no accompanying laptop. I wondered if the desk drawers had been searched, but I couldn't be sure.

I moved to the middle of the room and listened. Nothing. I didn't understand it. Epstein was clear that he'd be home the entire evening, and that I should stop by.

"Where are you?" I said out loud.

The room didn't talk, so I went back into the main room, wondering if I was missing something. I had a fleeting thought that I should call the police, but then dismissed it. I had no proof that anything bad had happened to Epstein, or that he was missing. He might show up at any time.

"Which means you need to leave," I muttered.

I moved to the door and checked out the peephole. The hall was quiet, so I eased the door open and slipped outside, then shut it carefully and headed down the hall. I didn't breathe until I was back on the street.

As I walked down my block, I had an eerie feeling I was being watched. I glanced around, but the night was dark, the only sound the traffic on adjoining streets. I looked for the Goofballs, but didn't see them. I thought I saw a light on at Shirley's house.

Must be Holly, I thought.

I stayed alert as I hurried around the side of my building. I paused and peeked around the corner, but didn't see anyone. I watched for a minute and then went up the stairs. When I let myself in, Willie was sitting on the couch in her terrycloth robe. Humphrey was asleep in her lap.

"He seems to be enjoying that soft robe," I said, pointing at the kitten.

She smiled. "Uh-huh."

Humphrey didn't move.

"Are you dead set on a rom-com?" I asked. "What about *The Damned Don't Cry*? Joan Crawford plays a woman who leaves her husband and the Texas oil fields and goes to New York."

"And she uses her feminine wiles to get ahead, and gets involved with a bad man, or a bad situation."

"You seem to know a lot about the movie."

"Hon, that's what happens in most of the film noir movies we watch."

"That's cold." I kicked off my shoes and came over to the couch.

She laughed. "I know there's more to the plots, but it sounds so heavy. How about something else?"

"Okay."

"How'd things go with Phil?"

"He wasn't there."

"Oh. Will you follow up with him tomorrow?"

"Yeah."

I snuggled up next to her and we watched *Knight and Day*, an action comedy with Tom Cruise and Cameron Diaz. I wasn't in tune with the movie, though. My mind wandered to Joan Crawford in *The Damned Don't Cry*. Was Shirley Durocher like Joan's character? Had she left Texas on the run, only to have her past come back to haunt her? My imagination may have gotten the best of me again, and so I tried to concentrate on the TV.

The movie eventually ended, and Willie and I went to bed. And even though I didn't know what we'd watched, the evening ended nicely.

CHAPTER THIRTEEN

The next morning, Willie and I lingered over breakfast. Since we both have hectic schedules and odd work hours, we try to fit in time for each other whenever we can. And this was one of those mornings. We fixed Denver omelets and hash browns, and lingered over coffee. While we ate, Humphrey entertained us by playing in an empty box. We have toys all over the condo for him, but he gets the biggest thrill crawling in and out of a box. Go figure.

After we finished, Willie left to take Humphrey to the vet for some shots. I showered, dressed, and went into my office. It was just after nine, and I figured Phil Epstein would be at work by then. I looked up the number for Doyle-Anderson Accounting, called and asked to speak with him.

"He hasn't come in yet," the receptionist said in a soft voice.

"When do you expect him?"

"He's usually here by now. I haven't heard that he called in sick, so I would expect him anytime. May I put you through to his voice mail?"

"That'd be great."

A moment later, Epstein's voice came on the line with a quick greeting. I left a message, asking him to call me as soon as he could, then hung up.

I stared at Humphrey Bogart on the *Big Sleep* poster. "Why isn't he there yet?"

Bogie didn't reply.

"Did something happen to Epstein?"

Bogie was still silent.

I thought for a minute, then picked up my phone again and called Detective Spillman.

"Oh, no," she said in greeting. "Do *not* tell me you're on this case."

I played innocent. "What case?"

"Cut it out. Are you looking into Shirley Durocher's murder?"

"Yes."

"Who hired you? The granddaughter?"

There was no fooling Spillman, so I didn't try. "Yes, Holly hired me."

A deep sigh carried through the phone. "What do you want from me?"

"A little information."

"You know I can't say much."

"I'll buy you a cup of coffee for your time."

There was a long silence. I could almost hear her arguing with herself. *Should she meet the charming detective? Would it hurt?*

"Fine," she finally said. "The Rooster in one hour."

"Thanks." I was grinning when I hung up.

I grabbed my keys, locked up, and went downstairs, then knocked on the Goofballs' door. Ace answered a moment later.

"Hey, Reed," he yawned.

"Sorry, did I wake you?"

He shook his head. "Nah, I was up. I have to work at ten,

and I was about to hop in the shower. Deuce is already at work."

"Did you find out anything last night?"

"No. We talked to a few people and then we decided to go to B 52s. No one saw or heard anything." He grimaced. "They mostly wanted to ask what Deuce and I knew about Shirley's murder. We can ask around some more tonight if you want."

"Sure," I said. "You never know who might've seen something."

"That's true. Detective Spillman was talking to some of the neighbors, too, and she said the same thing."

"Oh? She asked you about that night? Were you nervous talking to her?"

He puffed out his chest. "No, it was okay. She said if we wanted to wait until you were there, that'd be okay, but Deuce and I said we could talk to her. I kept telling myself I don't have anything to hide, and I just told the truth."

I patted his shoulder. "You are so right. Thanks for the help."

"Glad to." He rubbed a hand over his face. "Hey, I gotta get going."

"No problem, have a great day."

I thanked him again and then left for my meeting with Spillman. I was curious what she'd have to say about Shirley's death, and about her conversation with the Goofballs.

It took me fifteen minutes to weave through downtown to the Golden Triangle neighborhood, just south of downtown. I parked on Bannock near the Rooster & Moon Coffee Pub, a trendy little place that was near Spillman's precinct. Because of that, she frequently suggested it as a meeting place. As I got out of my car, my phone rang. I glanced at the number. Holly Durocher.

"Hey, I was going to call you with an update," I said.

"Oh, good. But I might have something for you."

"What's that?"

"I was at Shirley's last night. I was going through some paperwork and I found a few empty envelopes with a return address of Dallas, Texas."

"Did Shirley live there?" I asked as I crossed the street.

"No, she lived in Muleshoe."

"I only recently heard about Muleshoe."

"Yes." She laughed. "What a name for a town, right? But it's still interesting that she got mail from Texas. She always talked like she'd gotten out of there and had no interest in the state or anyone there. At first I thought the envelopes might be old, but I checked the meter stamps, and they were dated last month."

I paused outside the coffee shop. "Who were they from?"

"There was no name, just the return address, and it doesn't mean anything to me."

"Text it to me, and I'll do some research on it."

"Okay. I've got to go. Thanks for your help."

"Could I come by later and update you on what I've found out? I'm not sure what time."

"Sure. We're open until five, but I'm usually here later."

I ended the call, and walked into the Rooster. "Save It For Later" by The English Beat was playing, and I found myself humming to the tune while I waited in line. When I got to the front, I ordered a macchiato and went outside. It was cool, and I had no trouble finding a table. I sat down, tasted my drink, then pulled out my phone. Holly had texted me the address in Texas, and I looked it up online. After a bit of searching, I found a people-search site that told me a man named Bob Morrow lived at that address. The name meant nothing to me.

I sipped some coffee, then called Cal.

"O Great Detective, I did some research on Alan Prestwick," he said. "But I finished late last night, so I didn't call."

"No problem." I sipped some of my drink. "What'd you find out?"

"He and his wife filed for bankruptcy a few years ago. It looks like they've done better in the last year or two, but they aren't rich."

"Interesting. But if – and this is a stretch – Prestwick murdered Shirley for money, what money, and how would he get it?"

"Good point," he said drily. "I could ask Holly about it, if you want me to."

"Really? You've never wanted to talk to one of my clients before."

"Well ... uh ...."

"Come on, Cal, I know you like her."

"Yeah, but I'm just trying to be helpful."

I laughed. "I appreciate that. Can you do me another favor?"

"What's that?"

"See what you can find on Bob Morrow from Dallas, Texas." I gave him the address, and explained what Holly had found.

"Interesting. I've got to wrap up a few things with my client, and then I'll get on it. How soon do you need this?"

"Whenever you can get it. And can you meet me at her cupcake shop later this afternoon? I need to update her on what I've found."

"Why would I go?"

"So you get a chance to *talk* to her."

"Oh, yeah. Okay."

I shook my head. It was just as Willie had said. Cal would need help if he was going to ask Holly out on a date – provided she wasn't a killer.

"The shop closes at five, so it'll have to be before that."

I laughed again. "You looked up the shop hours?"

"Yeah."

He really was interested in this woman.

"One more thing. Did you find anything in Holly's past that might indicate she has or had a drug or alcohol problem?"

"No," he said slowly. "Does she?"

"Her mother said so, but I'm not sure I believe it."

"Me, either, but I'll do some checking."

"I've got some things to do today," I said, "but I'll call you later with a time."

"Great." With that, he ended the call.

I checked for messages, then put my phone away. A few minutes later, Spillman's blue Mustang came down the street. She parked down the block and walked back, came up to the table, and stared at me. At least I assumed she was staring at me: her dark sunglasses seemed to bore through me.

"How're you?" I asked.

She ran a hand through her blond hair. "Busy. I've only got a few minutes."

"Coffee?"

She nodded. I hurried inside and got her an espresso, her usual drink. When I came back to the table, she had sat down and was on her phone. She nodded and talked, and I pretended that I wasn't eavesdropping. But whatever she was talking about made no sense to me.

"What do you want to know?" she asked as she put her phone on the table.

"Have you found out how Shirley was killed?"

"Like I said, she suffered damage to her skull. It could've been with a blunt object. Someone hit her just right, and that's all it took. And no, the weapon was not found at her house, although there was some broken glass near her body."

"What broke?"

"I don't know."

I couldn't tell if she was holding back, but I knew better than to push her. "What time did she die?"

"Near as we can tell, sometime after midnight, maybe one in the morning."

"Do you have anyone with a clear motive?"

"Besides her granddaughter?"

I eyed her carefully. "You don't really think Holly's guilty, do you?"

"I have to look at everybody, Ferguson."

Her tone didn't convince me that she truly thought Holly was guilty. But then, I also knew she was right, and she had to look at everyone. Sometimes the most innocent-looking people were killers.

"Any other suspects?" I asked.

She tipped her head. "I still can't tell you that. And you? I'm sure you've been busy talking to people."

"I have, and no one's jumping out."

She gulped some espresso. "Isn't that the way it usually is?"

"Did alibis check out for Alan Prestwick and Phil Epstein?"

Her face didn't reveal anything. "Epstein doesn't have one. Prestwick, well ... it's his wife."

"And?"

"She says he was there all night."

"Do you believe her?"

Her expression didn't change. "I don't know what to think of her."

I sighed. "Okay, keeping it close to the vest."

She nodded, then tapped the table. "Are you holding back on anything?"

I briefly toyed with telling her about Phil Epstein, and that he didn't seem to be around, but I didn't really *know* anything other than that his condo had been unlocked the previous night. And if I did say something, I'd be incriminating myself for some kind of charge, so I nixed the idea.

"No," I said.

She stared at me. "I'm not sure I believe you."

I shrugged. "If I come up with anything, I'll let you know."

She downed the last of her espresso, grabbed her phone, and stood up.

"I have to go. Don't mess up my investigation."

I gave her a small salute. "I won't."

She gave me a wry smile and walked away. A minute later, her Mustang passed by on the street. She didn't look at me.

I finished my drink, then walked back to my car. Spillman hadn't told me much, but she left me wanting to talk to Prestwick's wife.

CHAPTER FOURTEEN

The Prestwicks lived a block away from our condo in a high-rise building of luxury townhomes, each with a balcony. I parked across the street and went into the building. Like the lobby in Epstein's building, this lobby had a bank of buzzers, each with a unit number next to it. I rang a buzzer for the Prestwicks' and waited. A long time later, a voice crackled through a speaker near the security door.

"Hello?"

"Mrs. Prestwick, this is Reed Ferguson. I belong to the same Homeowners Association as you, and I–"

That's as far as I got before she interrupted me.

"I know who you are. Come on up. I'm on the ninth floor."

The door buzzed, and then a click sounded. I grabbed the door and pulled it open, then crossed a small room to an elevator. I rode up to the ninth floor, got out, and looked around.

"This way." A woman with glasses peered out her doorway. "You're Reed?" she said as I approached.

"That's right."

I'd seen her once or twice when I'd gone to HOA meetings, and as I recalled, her curly hair had once been darker, but now it was brushed with gray. She was casually dressed in a long tee shirt and dark leggings, but it was a good look on her. It reminded me of something my mother would wear. But I doubted Prestwick's wife could do "miffed" like my mother did.

"Please come in," she said as she stepped aside. "I'm Wanda."

I slipped past her, then waited in a small foyer as she closed the door. She gestured with a finger for me to follow her, and we went around a corner that opened into a spacious living room. To the right was a kitchen done in expensive finishes. Expensive artwork adorned two of the walls.

"I was just having coffee on the balcony," she said as she walked past a couch and loveseat toward sliding glass doors. "May I serve you a cup?"

"No, thank you." I'd already had my fill of coffee this morning.

I followed her out onto the balcony, where she sat at a small glass-topped table. The Prestwicks' unit faced east, so they did not have a mountain view. Too bad.

She sat down and indicated I should sit in a chair across from her. She picked up a brightly colored mug and took a sip. The chill in the air didn't seem to bother her. She looked at me over the edge of the mug.

"You're investigating Shirley Durocher's death, aren't you?"

I nodded. "Did your husband tell you that?"

"No, but the police were here asking where he was the night she died."

I wondered why Prestwick hadn't mentioned my investigation to his wife, but I kept that to myself.

"You don't seem upset that they're checking up on your husband."

Her shoulders lifted slightly. "No. Apparently he'd had words with Shirley the night of the HOA meeting, and so the police were looking into that. It's routine."

"And?"

She set her mug down with a clink on the glass table. "Alan came home from the meeting, and he was with me all night."

"No chance he went out?"

"No," she said firmly. "He came home, we watched the late news, and we went to bed." She looked away. "It's silly to suspect him."

"Did your husband have any problems with Shirley?"

She snickered. "Who didn't?"

I frowned. "That seems to be the general consensus."

She gazed to the east. The faint sounds of traffic from Eighteenth Avenue drifted up to us. "Shirley would call here at various times, asking Alan one thing or another. Sometimes he'd have to meet with her to discuss things. If he didn't, she'd keep badgering him until he gave in. I don't want to speak ill of the dead, but Shirley could be a very frustrating woman. Most of her complaints were unwarranted. I'm sure you've heard some of them. She wasn't an easy woman to deal with, but she thought the HOA had the power to control everything, and that Alan wielded that power."

I thought about Shirley's leaf-cleanup request. "Yes." Then something else occurred to me. "How often did your husband meet with Shirley?"

She chose her words carefully. "A time or two."

"Did her behavior upset your husband?"

I got another hard look.

"You mean upset enough to murder her?" she asked.

I gave her a little inquisitive shrug.

"No, he wasn't *that* upset," she said. "Alan wouldn't hurt a fly."

I circled back around to the night of the HOA meeting. "The police asked you about Alan's argument with Shirley after the meeting?"

"Yes, that's correct."

"Did you ask Alan about it?"

She glanced away. "Yes."

"What did he tell you?"

"They were fighting about Phil Epstein."

She wasn't forthcoming with information. "What exactly?" I asked.

"Shirley had accused Phil of stealing some of the HOA money," she finally said, "and Alan said he wasn't sure there was any proof of that. Alan knew he was going to have to talk to Phil about it, and he didn't want to."

"Why is that?"

She looked at me again. "Alan and Phil did not get along. They're both pigheaded, and sometimes they argue about the management of the HOA, or what decisions need to be made."

I hadn't heard that before. I'd have to follow up with both men about that.

"How did Alan handle all these issues with Shirley?" I asked. "Did he ever get angry with her?"

"Not that I'm aware of, but I was never with him when he talked to her."

"How well did you know Shirley?"

"Not very well. I'd see her at the HOA meetings, and sometimes afterward, when she'd want to talk to Alan."

Her tone bordered on harsh.

I stared at her. "You didn't like her?"

"I wasn't fond of her."

"Do you know of anyone who might've wanted to harm her? Any enemies?"

She picked up her mug and took a sip. "No, not really."

"Are you sure?"

"Yes. I just feel bad because I don't ... didn't particularly like her. But someone who treated others the way she did – who knows who might've wanted to ... murder her."

I glanced around. "This is a nice place."

She nodded. "Yes. We've been here a long time, and I'm glad we're staying."

I arched an eyebrow.

"We ..." She hesitated. "You probably heard this from Alan. We ran into some financial trouble a while back. I had to work longer than I'd planned to, for the extra money. But it all worked out. I only recently retired."

Alan hadn't told me any of that, but I wasn't going to say so. "Oh? What did you do?"

"I worked at Qwest. Well, it's CenturyLink now. I had a good job there. It was a frustrating company to work for, but my salary was good." She waved a hand around. "I don't miss it."

"That's nice," I murmured. I looked around again. The Prestwicks had good taste. "You've heard about the problems with thieves in the neighborhood?"

She nodded. "Things are being stolen out of some cars."

"Have you been a victim?"

"No."

Just then, a house phone rang. She glanced back toward the living room.

"I really should go," she said as she scooted back her chair and stood up. "Would you excuse me?"

"Of course."

I followed her inside, where she went into the kitchen and picked up a phone. I tried to signal her that I would let myself out, but she held up a finger to indicate I should wait.

"Yes, that's fine," she was saying.

I glanced around while she talked. The kitchen was orderly and sparsely decorated. My gaze fell to some prescription bottles on the counter near where I stood. I admit, I was curious. Wanda had her back to me, so I reached out and turned one of the bottles. It was a Valium prescription. I couldn't tell if the prescription was for her or Alan, and was about to check when she turned back to me. I looked toward the deck, hoping I didn't have a guilty look on my face.

"I'll see you soon." Wanda hung up the phone and looked at me. "I do need to go soon."

I jerked a thumb toward the entrance. "I was going to let myself out."

"Alan had nothing to do with Shirley's death."

"Okay," I said, not sure how to respond. "I certainly thank you for your time." I pulled out a business card and handed it to her. "If you think of anything else that might be important, would you give me a call?"

She took it, her lips pinched distastefully. "The police asked me to do the same thing." She set the card down on the counter near the prescription bottle. "I frankly don't think I'll have any more information, but I'll keep you in mind."

I turned around and started through the living room, then glanced over my shoulder. Wanda was headed toward me. I looked at the counter, and the prescription bottles weren't in sight. Wanda walked past me and showed me to the door. I started to thank her, but the door was already closed.

I walked slowly to the elevator, thinking it hadn't been just the balcony air that was cool. Wanda had been as well. I wasn't sure what that was about. Was she just defensive of her husband? I'm sure it was uncomfortable to talk to Detective Spillman and me about him. Or was there more? Prestwick *did* have an argument with Shirley, so he bore scrutiny, even if he wasn't a likely suspect.

The elevator arrived and I rode it down to the lobby. I wasn't entirely convinced that Wanda had been completely forthright with me. I wasn't sure what I was missing, or if it meant that Alan Prestwick had murdered Shirley, but I was going to find out.

CHAPTER FIFTEEN

I still needed to follow up on Karen Durocher's alibi, so I decided to do that next. Karen had said she frequented Buddy's Bar. It was located on Colfax, near Kipling Street. Then I remembered that when I'd called the bar yesterday, they'd told me that the bartender, Paul Kava, wouldn't be in until noon today.

I glanced at my watch. That left me about an hour, so I headed to a Subway and got some lunch. While I was there, I called Phil Epstein's office, but he wasn't in. I asked the receptionist if she was still expecting him, and she said yes, but this time there seemed to be the slightest hesitation. She put me through to his voice mail again, and I left him another message. Then I put away my phone, went out to the 4-Runner, and headed to Buddy's Bar.

At 12:30, I was parked down the street from the bar, which was in a nondescript red-brick building. I almost missed the place, until I saw the tiny sign above the door that read "Buddy's." I walked inside and let my eyes adjust to the dim light that filtered in from two windows that faced Colfax. A few people were eating at tables, and an older man perched on a stool at the bar. I expected music, but there wasn't any. The whole aura of the place was quiet and depressing.

I sauntered up to the bar, took a seat at one end, and glanced at the old man. He stared at me with lifeless eyes, then picked up his beer and took a hefty drink. He had the look of a "regular." I gave him a little nod, and he returned it with one of his own. A muscle-bound bartender came through a door at the other end of the bar. He saw me and walked over, towering over me as he took my order.

"What'll you have?" His voice was surprisingly high-pitched.

"A Coke."

He gave me an odd look.

"I'm here for business," I said, then flashed my private investigator's license quickly, hoping he'd think I was a cop. "Are you Paul Kava?"

"Yeah. What do you want?" he asked as he grabbed a glass and filled it with ice and Coke.

"A little information."

"Okay." He handed me the Coke, then started wiping down the bar with a white cloth.

That was too easy. I studied him, and he waited for me to continue.

"Can you tell me if Karen Durocher was here a week ago, on Monday night?" I asked.

"Karen? Yeah, she was."

"You're sure?"

He nodded. "She's here most nights." Then he stopped wiping the bar, and a sly smile crossed his face.

"What?" I said.

"Karen said a guy might come in here asking about her, and whether she was here that night."

THE DAMNED DON'T DIE

"Oh?"

"You're following up on her mother's death, right? And you're wondering if Karen did it."

I nodded. "Karen didn't have any secrets from you."

"Nope."

"Does that mean she was asking for you to lie for her?"

He put big hands on the bar, and I noticed how thick his forearms were. Now that I was paying more attention to him, I realized that everything about him was big, from his legs to his arms and his thick chest and neck. I wouldn't want to meet him in the wrong place.

He put his face close to mine. "You might think that, but it would be a mistake."

I leaned back, just a little. "No problem." I puffed up my chest, trying to appear tough as well, but he didn't seem to notice. I doubted anyone scared him.

"Besides that, there were a number of regulars in here that night, and they can all tell you Karen was here."

"Maybe I'll talk to them."

He shook his head. "Don't go bothering anyone in here, all right?"

"Okay. Why're *you* talking to me?"

He shrugged. "I don't want any trouble. I talk to you, then you'll beat it." There was a not-so-subtle hint in his tone.

"Hey, Paul," the regular at the other end of the bar said. "How about another?"

"Hang on," Paul said to me.

He went to the old man, served him a beer, said something in a low tone, then came back to me.

"What else do you want to know?" he asked.

"How long have you known Karen?"

"Known her? I don't know her, just talk to her here at the bar, just like I do with all the other people that come in here.

119

Didn't you know, that's what bartenders do, we listen." I waited for him to continue. "She's fine. She hangs out with Fred quite a bit."

"Fred? That's her boyfriend?"

"I don't know if he's her boyfriend or not."

I stared at him. "So she was hooking up with other guys?"

"Maybe a time or two, but lately it's been Fred."

"Who're some of these other guys?"

He pursed his lips. "I'm not telling you that, and you're not going to bug them. All I will say is that Karen and Fred are in here quite a bit, hanging out and drinking. They were in here that night you're asking about."

"When did they leave?"

"Not until we closed at midnight."

"You were here until then? That's a long day for you."

"So?" His eyes narrowed. "And to answer your question, yeah, I'm sure."

"You're not really telling me what you know about her," I said pointedly.

He crossed his arms, and the muscles flexed. "She sits in here a lot, and the more she drinks, the more she talks, mostly about needing money."

I waved a hand around. "Booze costs money."

"Fred pays. You going to let me finish?"

"Sorry." I took a sip of Coke and waited. "So she needs money."

"Yeah. From what I can tell, she hasn't had the easiest life. She's had a lot of jobs, and she hasn't made great choices. You hear things, you know? People complain, you hear everything."

"Did you ever meet her mother?"

"Shirley?"

"That's right. Was she ever in here?"

"No, but Karen talked about her an awful lot, and she wasn't too fond of her mother."

"Why is that?"

"She made it sound like her mom was a bitch. I had to laugh because a lot of people feel that way about their mothers, but what're you going to do? I'd say 'maybe your old man was mean to her,' because I get a lot of that kind of talk in here. But Karen would say she didn't remember much of her dad, that she hardly knew him, and she blamed her mom for that, too."

He was an armchair psychologist. But he was talking, which was good. "What else?"

"She thought something happened between Shirley and her dad, but Karen never knew exactly what. It's the kind of drunken talk that people do."

"Did Karen talk about her daughter?"

"Yeah, mostly that they didn't see each other very often." He smiled, this time ruefully. "It's funny, the stories you hear. Karen was blaming her mother for things, and how they didn't get along, but she didn't see the problems with her own daughter." He shrugged again. "But people that come in here aren't the type to look in the mirror, if you know what I mean."

"Did Karen tell you that she thinks Holly might've had something to do with her mother's death?"

"I don't know anything about that."

He was talking, and I kept asking questions. "From what you know of Karen, do you think she's angry enough at her mom to murder her?"

He thought about that. "For the most part, Karen's pretty easygoing, kidding with other people at the bar. Until she's had a little too much, and she starts thinking about money. Then that leads her into being mad at her mom. But angry enough to kill? I don't think so."

I took another drink. "You said the boyfriend's name is Fred?"

He held up a finger. "I didn't say he was a boyfriend."

"Okay, the guy she was hanging out with. Fred. Do you know where he lives?"

He shook his head. "I don't get *that* familiar with folks in here."

"Okay, when will Fred be in here again?"

He frowned. "I don't want you bugging people in here."

"Yeah, but I need to talk to him."

"No, you don't."

"How about letting me make that call?"

His eyes narrowed, and the big forearms came back onto the bar. "Why didn't Karen tell you how to find him?"

I scratched my chin. "I don't know."

"Well, you're not going to wait here to talk to him." He picked up the white cloth. "I know you're trying to find a murderer, but it's not Karen." He pointed toward the door. "I think you need to go now."

"Okay."

I reached for my wallet.

"The Coke's on me. Just mosey on out of here."

I thanked him and headed for the door. As I was about to go out, a man in jeans with a plaid jacket and green baseball cap came through the door.

"Hey, hey!" he said loudly.

The old man sitting at the bar turned and waved a wobbly hand. "Fred, get over here. Your beer's getting cold."

I glanced over my shoulder. Paul gave me a hard look, as if to warn me from saying anything to Fred. I didn't want any trouble with him, so I left, knowing that Fred would have to come out at some point, and I could talk to him then.

I walked outside and down the street to the 4-Runner. While I waited, I called Alan Prestwick. He barely greeted me.

"Have you had a chance to talk to Phil Epstein?" I asked.

"Not yet. I left him a message, but he hasn't returned my call."

"Mine, either. Do you know where he is?"

"At work, I guess."

"I hear you didn't get along with him."

A heavy breath rattled through the phone. "So what? He and I didn't always see things the same way, but we managed to get things done for the HOA."

"Did you ever see him tell Shirley Durocher off?"

"No. You talked to my wife," he abruptly changed the subject.

"That's right."

"What'd she tell you?"

"That you were home with her all night."

"Are you satisfied I didn't have anything to do with Shirley's murder?"

"Not entirely."

Silence for a moment, and then he cleared his throat.

"Why isn't that good enough for you?"

"Call it a gut feeling," I said. "There's something more there."

"I can assure you there's not."

The line went dead. I could picture him slamming his office phone down. I put my phone away, turned up "Meat Is Murder," a CD by the Smiths, an alternative band I love, and watched the bar. The afternoon dragged on, and I grew bored. I texted Willie and said I didn't know when I'd be home, and that I'd touch base with her later. Then I texted Cal to let him know I wasn't sure when I'd be available later in the day, but I'd call when I could go to the cupcake shop and to call me with what he found out about Bob Morrow and Holly.

Finally, a little before three o'clock, Fred emerged from the bar. I started to get out of my car, but he hurried to a beat-up Dodge truck that was sitting in front of the building and got in. He pulled onto Colfax and I followed him.

CHAPTER SIXTEEN

Fred drove to Wadsworth Boulevard and went south. I did my usual, and let several cars get between his truck and my 4-Runner. He drove fast, and when he reached Jewell Avenue, he turned east and drove into a large parking lot by an old building that I guessed had once been a Safeway grocery store. Now it had a big "Bingo" sign in the window, announcing that bingo was every Wednesday afternoon and on Fridays and Saturdays.

"Hmm," I said to myself as I pulled in after Fred. "Fred plays bingo?" I wouldn't have pictured that, but then, I didn't know the guy.

He hopped out of the truck, adjusted his baseball cap, and patted his jacket pockets. As he started inside, I got out of the 4-Runner.

"Fred?" I called out.

He turned around slowly and his eyes squinted just a bit in curiosity. "Yeah?"

I started toward him. "Could I have a moment of your time?"

"Well, hurry up." He beckoned with his hand for me to catch up to him. "I'm already late."

I trotted after him. When he got to the door, a few people who were smoking waved and said hello to him. Fred exchanged quick pleasantries with them, then scooted inside, where a man at the door greeted him by name.

"About time you got here," he said.

Fred nodded. "I know."

The big room had several long tables in rows that faced a small stage at the back of the room. Most of the tables were full, and the buzz of conversation filled the air.

"Come on," Fred said to me.

I followed him to a booth near the back corner of the room. He bought three bingo cards, then glanced at me.

"You want in?"

I shook my head.

"Suit yourself. You're missing out."

"I just need a moment before you get started."

"Talk to me while we're playing. I ain't missing out on any more games. Besides, I'll bet I know who you are."

"Is that so?"

"Yeah. Karen said some guy might be coming around, asking questions, and so did Paul."

"You can't fool everyone," I said.

"No, sir."

Before I could say another word, he hurried to a table near the back, pulled a few thick colored pens from his coat pocket, and sat down. He jerked his head for me to sit next to him. At the other end of the table were two old ladies, one with thick glasses, the other with big hearing aids. They both were done up, their hair and lipstick perfect. They both smiled and greeted Fred warmly.

"Fred, this game's almost over," the lady with the glasses said as she peered closely at her bingo cards. "You hang tight for a minute."

On the stage, a man was pulling balls from a bingo cage and calling the numbers into a microphone. With each number, the room erupted in chatter.

"All right, Dorothy," Fred said to her. Then he tipped his chair back, hooked his thumbs in his pockets, and looked at me. "What do you need to know?"

I took a moment to gather my thoughts. "So Karen's told you that I'm investigating her mother's murder," I said in low voice.

I was worried the ladies would hear what we were talking about, but they were paying attention to the game and hardly seemed to notice us.

"Uh-huh."

"Karen's daughter Holly is worried about it. The police seem to think she might've had something to do with her grandmother's death. Quite frankly, it sounds as if Karen may have helped put some of the blame on Holly."

He turned to me, surprised. "That's not a nice thing for Karen to do."

I nodded. "You're right."

More bingo numbers were called, and the old ladies kept at their game.

He stared past me. "That's just downright cold. I'm estranged from my own daughter, and you can't imagine what I'd give for some time with her." His brow crinkled. "You don't want to spend that time thinking ill of someone."

"Have you ever met Holly?"

"No, I never had the pleasure. Karen's talked about her some." He pursed his lips. "She sounds like quite a gal. Karen said she was helping out her grandmother, and as far as I'm concerned, there's a lot to be said for that."

"What does she say about Holly?"

"She doesn't speak highly of her. I don't know what that's all about, but from what I can tell, Holly's done well for herself with that cupcake shop. I don't know what Karen's beef is."

"How well do you know Karen?"

"Ah, we probably go back about a year or so."

"How long have you been dating her?"

The legs of his chair slowly met the floor, and he gave me a sidelong look.

"I'm not dating anybody," he murmured, clearly not wanting anyone to hear this part of our discussion.

Suddenly someone shouted "Bingo," and everyone looked in the direction of the voice. Fred partially stood up and craned his neck to see.

"Jane Totino," he said with a little smile. "Good for her."

The other two ladies looked at Fred.

"Maybe you'll bring us some luck," said the woman with the hearing aids. "We haven't won all afternoon."

"Let's hope so." Fred grinned. "Here's a little luck to both of you." Then he blew them a kiss.

I restrained a smile at Fred and his flirtations.

"What do you think about Karen?" I asked.

He shrugged. "We have a nice time together."

"Nothing more?"

He shook his head. "Just friends."

I was sure there was more there, but I was too polite to say so.

"Do you think Karen would do anything bad to her mother?" I went on.

"I don't think so. She doesn't strike me as that type."

"Paul said when Karen got drunk, she could get pretty morose, and she didn't speak kindly of her mother."

"That's true. I guess her mother could be difficult, but

Karen's talk was just that – talk. Kill her mother? Nah. If Karen was going to kill anyone, it'd be her daddy."

"Why do you say that?"

"That's who she was angry with. I guess he took off when Karen was little, took all their money and was gone. If you ask me, that's what made Shirley bitter and angry. You're on your own with a young daughter and you have bills to pay. She had to bust her ass to make ends meet. That'd be hard on anybody." He arranged his cards as a new game began. "If there was a reason why Shirley was a miser, it'd be that. Karen said Shirley held on to her money, and that made Karen upset. I think Karen went to her mom a time or two for a loan, and Shirley wouldn't give it to her. Karen was mad about that."

"Did she ask Holly for a loan, too?"

"I don't know about that, but it wouldn't surprise me. And if Holly turned Karen down, that would've upset her, too." He looked to the front of the room. "Hold on. Another game's starting."

The announcer wished everyone luck, and then the game began. Somehow Fred managed to listen to the numbers being called and talk with me at the same time.

"Do you know Shirley's husband's name?"

"Karen's daddy?" He shook his head as he marked one of his cards. "I don't recall her ever mentioning it."

"Did you ever meet Shirley?"

"A time or two. She stopped by Karen's house when I was there. She seemed nice enough, but I don't think they talked much. I don't know why. It's a shame. I'm telling you, I've had my share of distance from my family. That's one thing I don't understand about Karen, why she thought her mother owed her money or would give her an inheritance when they weren't close, and Karen wasn't that friendly to her. That made Karen angry, but she should've made it right with her mom, regardless."

"Was Karen mad at her mom a lot?"

The pen paused over one of the cards. "Not usually."

I let that sink in. "Karen says she was with you at the bar the night of the murder."

"That's right." His voice was low. "We were there until it closed. And just like Paul told you, we got plenty of witnesses. I can give you their names." Then he gave me another sidelong look. "Besides that, we were at her house the rest of the night." He winked.

"No offense, but you could be lying."

Now he turned to face me, and gave me an appraising look. "I could be, but I'm not."

If he'd taken offense, he didn't show it. He just appeared very confident in his statement as he continued marking up his cards as numbers matched his squares.

"Did Karen ever say who she thought might've murdered her mother?"

"Besides Holly?" He shook his head in disgust. "No, but Karen said her mother was worried about someone being around the house." He shrugged again. "I didn't pay too much attention. Maybe whoever that was had something to do with her murder."

"Does the name Bob Morrow mean anything to you?"

He rubbed his chin. "Can't say that it does."

"Come on, pay attention," the woman with the glasses chided Fred.

"I've got it going." He pointed with the pen at one of the cards. "I'm one away from bingo on this one. If I get it, I'll buy you a drink."

She smiled at him, and he winked again at me.

"I got to concentrate now," he said to me. "I've told you all I can."

"You've been very helpful." I pushed back my chair and got up. "Thanks for your time."

"No problem."

By the time I reached the door, someone had again called "bingo," and the place erupted.

I mulled over the conversation as I walked back to my car. I still wasn't convinced that Karen was innocent, and I needed to talk to her again. I got in, pulled out my cell phone, and called Cal. It went to voice mail. I grimaced as I started the 4-Runner and drove out of the parking lot.

CHAPTER SEVENTEEN

When Karen Durocher opened the door, she was in a bathrobe with a drink in her hand, and she looked at me with tired eyes.

"What do you want?" She spoke carefully as she put a hand out to hold the screen door open, then leaned against the door jamb.

"Did Fred tell you I was coming by?"

"No, he–" She suddenly stopped, realizing that I'd figured out who she'd been dating. "Oh, you know about him, huh?"

"Yep."

She held up her glass in a mock toast. "Well, good for you, honey."

Her bathrobe could've been cinched a little tighter, and I kept my eyes on her face. Did I detect more stress lines than I'd noticed before?

"You're not going out tonight?" I asked.

"Maybe later."

I glanced around. "You want to talk on the porch or can I come in?"

She looked past me at a car going down the street. "You might as well come in," she said. She turned around and disappeared back into the house.

I grabbed the screen door before it could shut and let myself in. She took a seat at the couch, crossed one leg over the other, exposing a decent amount of thigh. Then she gave me an appraising look.

"What have you found out?" she asked.

I went and sat in the same blue recliner and returned the look.

She took a sip of her drink. "Well?"

"I don't think you murdered your mother."

"I was a suspect, huh?"

I nodded.

"Fred said I was with him all night?"

"Yes," I said. "He and Paul at the bar said plenty of people saw you there and that you stayed until it closed." I ran a hand over my jaw. "I could take the time to talk to all of them, but for now, I'm going to trust you all."

"Isn't that charitable of you."

"But I also don't think Holly had anything to do with her grandmother's death."

She pursed her lips but didn't reply.

"Tell me something," I said. "Do you honestly think your own daughter would commit murder, or are you angry at her for not lending you money?"

I received a hard glare for that.

"Who told you I was trying to get a loan from Holly?" she finally asked.

"Who do you think?"

"Fred." She frowned. "All right, that's true. I tried to get some money from Holly, but she wouldn't do it."

"You also tried to get money out of Shirley, but she didn't loan you any, either."

She nodded. "That doesn't mean I killed her."

"I didn't say you did, but others might wonder."

"I don't know that Holly would've done anything to her grandmother, but I didn't tell the police that. It was more that they were already looking in that direction because Holly is going to get all of my mother's money."

"But you didn't discourage their thinking."

She shook her head, and for the first time I saw a hint of something other than anger there. I put my hands on my knees and leaned forward.

"Let's get down to some real business," I said. "Do you have any idea who might've killed your mother?"

She looked away. "I don't know."

I pointed at her glass. "Why don't you climb out of that booze and think for a minute?"

"I don't know," she repeated.

I studied her for a long time. "This is what I'm hearing, that you're angry at your father just as much as at Shirley. He's the one you've been bitter toward all these years."

She met my gaze, and her eyes were wet. "He didn't treat us well. All I remember is them fighting. Then he left one day and never came back. Do you know what that's like to have your father abandon you?"

I shook my head. "No."

"It's hard. You wonder about it, and you blame yourself."

"You think Holly's been doing some of that with her own father gone? And on top of that, she has you angry at her?"

"I–" Her jaw snapped shut.

"You didn't think about that, did you?"

"No," she whispered.

"I'm no therapist, but maybe you need to straighten some things out before you start pointing the finger elsewhere."

"Is this part of your investigation?"

"Call it free advice."

A long, uncomfortable silence filled the room. I'd rarely been that blunt with someone before, but I couldn't hold back. Then I switched subjects.

"Who would be contacting Shirley from Dallas?"

"I don't know."

"Did she have relatives or friends there? Anyone you know? Her ex?"

"I don't know."

"What's your father's name?"

She shook her head. "I don't remember hearing it, and Mother never said."

"Never? Come on."

"No, it's true. She didn't speak of him much at all, and she wouldn't mention him by name."

"Does the name Bob Morrow mean anything to you?"

"No." Then her eyes narrowed slightly.

"What?"

"I just remembered something."

I waited.

"A week or two before her death, Mother was over here. She was worried."

"About what?"

"Someone was coming around the house."

"A few people have said that. She was afraid that the thieves in the neighborhood might be targeting her house."

"No, it was more." Her face pinched in concern. "I asked her about the thieves, and she said it wasn't that. I think she said something about 'him,' but I didn't know what she meant.

She said he might've come back, and I asked who she meant, and she told me never mind, and that was it."

"Do you remember anything else?"

"No."

"Why didn't you tell me this before?"

"It just came to mind." She glanced at her glass.

"You were drunk."

"Maybe a little. What're you going to make of it?"

That flash of tenderness was gone, and she was back to bitter and angry.

I thought for a moment. "Your mother had plenty of money, but it didn't appear that she was getting that much from her pension and Social Security."

"She always had money."

"So you and Holly said. But she never had another job, something off the books?"

She shook her head. "Not that I know of."

"And you don't know of anyone else who might've wanted her dead?"

"You already asked me that," she snapped.

"Yeah," I replied, almost as heated as she was, "and you've already remembered things that you didn't before."

She raised a hand dismissively. "If I think of anything else, I'll tell you."

I sat back. "I'm going to find your mother's killer. I don't think it was Holly, or you. But we need to get to the bottom of this." I stood up. "Do you still have my card?"

She jerked a thumb behind her. "It's in the kitchen."

"If you think of anything else, you call me."

"Okay."

I crossed the room and let myself out, and she stayed in the chair, sipping her drink. When I got outside, I took a deep breath. Then I called Cal as I walked to my car. This time he answered.

"I'm going to head over to the cupcake shop and talk to Holly," I said. "Want to meet me there?"

"Sure, but guess what I just found out."

"What?"

"I was finishing some research for you on that address in Dallas."

"And?"

He was stretching out his reveal. "It belongs to a guy named Bob Morrow."

"That's what I told you earlier," I said as I slid behind the wheel of the 4-Runner.

"Sure, but you're never going to believe who this guy was married to, way back when."

I almost dropped the phone as it dawned on me. "Shirley Durocher."

"Yep."

"She kept her maiden name?"

"It looks that way. It took me a while to find their marriage record. Turns out the county they were married in doesn't keep online records, and I had to make some calls."

That was interesting. Normally with Cal, if he couldn't find the information on the internet, he was done. This time, he was going over and above what he usually did for me. "Good work. So Shirley's ex has been contacting her recently."

"Someone from that house has. If not her ex, then his new wife."

"What's her name?"

"Gail."

"How long have they been married?"

"Over thirty years."

"Huh." I stared out the windshield. "I wonder what Bob Morrow is up to."

"I don't know, but I need to leave so I can meet you at Holly's shop."

He abruptly ended the call.

I sat for a long time, mulling things over. Then I called Phil Epstein at his condo, but he didn't answer. He was doing a good job of avoiding me. I left a message, then started the car and headed west to Golden.

CHAPTER EIGHTEEN

Sunshine Cupcakes was located a block off of Washington Avenue, the main street in Golden. Golden originated as a gold-rush town, but now is a lively small city with lots of restaurants, shops, and museums, not to mention Coors Brewery. I hadn't been to Golden in a long time, and I was surprised at how many people were in the downtown area. As I parked in a covered garage near the shop, I told myself that when the case was finished, I'd ask Willie if she'd like to visit Woody's, a fun pizza joint on the main street, for dinner. Then we could walk around town and visit the shops. She'd enjoy that.

As I got out of the 4-Runner, Cal drove into the garage in his beat-up Honda Civic.

"Don't you think it's time to retire that car?" I asked as he got out.

"It's a classic," he said with a smile.

Cal could well afford a better car, but this was just one more of his eccentricities.

"Did you find out anything about HOA finances?"

"Yes. There's nothing special there. I can't see where Epstein was stealing money."

"Good work," I said.

As we headed for the cupcake shop, I scrutinized him.

"What?" he finally asked.

"Look at you. Your hair is neatly combed, you wore something other than a T-shirt, and your clothes aren't wrinkled. If I didn't know better, I'd say you were visiting with a client."

"So?"

I grinned. "You're trying to make a good impression on Holly."

"We *are* meeting a client."

"Uh-huh."

"I'm just trying to help you."

"And I appreciate that," I said. "Are you going to ask her out?"

He stopped. "What? Who me?"

I nodded.

He stared at me. "I wouldn't know how. What would I say?"

"Ask her how her day's been, and pay her a compliment."

"Like what?"

Willie was right. He was going to need lots of help.

"Tell her she looks nice, or you're impressed with the shop, something like that."

"I don't know if I can do that." He adjusted his collar and took a deep breath.

"Just don't die on me," I muttered as we went around the corner.

When we walked into the store, Holly was behind a long glass display counter, busy with a woman who was holding a little girl's hand. Holly made eye contact with me, and said pleasantly, "I'll be with you in a moment."

"Sure," Cal and I both said at once.

I looked around. The room was a rectangle, with a few small round tables across from the counter. I stepped up to the display case and studied the assortment of cupcakes: vanilla cream with raspberry, chocolate peanut butter, cookies and cream, mint chocolate, snickerdoodle, double chocolate, and more. Their sweet aroma tickled my nose, and my mouth watered.

We waited, and Holly finished putting cupcakes into a big box as she chatted with her customer.

"This'll be perfect for the birthday party tonight," the woman said.

"I hope they enjoy the cupcakes," Holly replied.

Holly handed the box to the woman, then went to the end of the counter and rang up the order. She waved at the woman and the girl as they went out the door.

"Hang on a second," she said to us.

She spun around and went through a door at the other end of the counter, then returned with a young woman in an apron.

"Sarah, watch things up here while I talk to these guys," Holly said.

"Sure thing."

Sarah fixed Cal and me with a curious gaze as we followed Holly through the door and into the kitchen in the back. More cupcakes sat on a long table, and a mixer had a light-colored batter in it. Empty cupcake pans sat next to the mixer.

"How's your day?" Cal blurted out.

I glanced at him, willing him to calm himself. *Be cool.*

Holly looked down timidly. "It's good."

"Is now a good time to talk?" I asked.

She nodded. "It's been busy, with lots of orders for parties, but Sarah can handle things out front for a few minutes." She finally looked up at me. "How have things been going?"

I grimaced. "I still haven't caught a murderer, but I'm beginning to wonder about your grandfather coming back into the picture."

Her eyes went wide. "What?"

"Bear with me for a moment," I went on. "Do you have the envelopes here?"

"Sure, hang on a second."

She went over to a bag that was sitting on a desk in the corner of the kitchen. She pulled two envelopes from it and handed them to me.

"Here."

I studied them, then passed them to Cal.

"Nothing in them," Cal observed. "And nothing unusual about the envelopes."

"Right," Holly said. "That's what I told Reed."

Cal waved the envelopes in the air. He was on a roll, and I let him have his moment. He deserved it. "But this address is for Bob Morrow."

"Yes?"

"That's your grandfather."

"Really? How do you know that?" She stared at him.

"I looked up the address online and did some research."

"Um ..." she gulped.

"What?" I asked.

She was pale. "I also found this in one of the envelopes."

She handed me a paper with a handwritten note in block letters that read, "We need to talk. I'm tired of what you're doing to me. It ends now." The scrawled signature looked like 'Bob', although the 'B' looked more like a 'D' or maybe an 'R'."

I showed it to Cal.

"From Morrow?" he asked.

"A pretty good bet," I said. "And he's threatening Shirley."

"Oh, no." Holly put a hand to her mouth. "You don't think ..." Her voice trailed off.

Cal and I didn't say anything.

"What do you know about my grandfather?" she asked.

"Morrow has been remarried for thirty years," Cal said, "and he worked in the oil fields. He lives in Dallas."

"Did he have kids with this woman?"

Cal shook his head. "No."

"Is he … um … is he a criminal or anything like that?" she asked. "Shirley hated him, you know."

"Not that I could find," Cal said.

"Huh." She pursed her lips.

I was watching Holly as Cal talked. Everything that he shared seemed brand new to her. Cal handed the envelopes back to her, and she scrutinized them carefully, then laid them on the table.

Cal cleared his throat and adjusted his collar again, so I took over the conversation. "You never met your grandfather, right?"

"No. Grandmother and my mother rarely mentioned him. I always figured he was dead."

"He's alive and living in Texas," I said. "Your grandmother never talked about any of this?"

She shook her head. "It's all news to me. But why would he be sending her letters?"

"We don't know what he sent her," I said, "but I'd like to talk to him and see if he knows anything about your grandmother's death."

"You think he had something to do with Grandmother's murder? But why?"

"I don't know, but I intend to find out." I gazed at her. "Your mother seems very bitter toward him."

"Yeah. The only thing she ever said was that he … Bob … took what little money they had and ran off, leaving Grandmother and my mom without a penny. That made things really difficult."

I thought for a second. "Your mother said one of the last times she saw Shirley, she was concerned about 'him' coming back."

"Who?" Holly asked.

"That's the question." I gestured at the envelopes. "Was it Morrow?"

She didn't say anything.

"Have you talked to the police anymore?"

"Not a word."

"And you're continuing to go through your grandmother's things?"

She nodded. "I was there last night for a little bit."

"When did you leave?"

"Around 8:30."

I tipped my head. "Are you sure about that?"

"Yes, why?"

I frowned. "I thought I saw you there, but it was later, after nine."

"No, I was home by then."

"Hmm."

"Someone was at my grandmother's house?" Now alarm filled her voice.

"I'm not sure," I said, "but you should check the house, just in case. I'll keep an eye on it, too."

"Thanks."

She leaned back against a stainless-steel refrigerator. "You really think my grandfather has come back around?"

I shrugged. "I have to consider everything. I'm going to call him and have a little chat."

Holly glanced at Cal, then back at me. "Um, has my mother been a pain?"

"She's interesting, to say the least."

"I still can't believe she was trying to put the blame for my grandmother's death on me."

"Well," I said slowly.

"What?" she asked.

"I think that's been exaggerated a bit, although your mother didn't do you any favors when she didn't even try to convince the police that you *wouldn't* do such a thing."

She nodded sadly. "That does sound like her, unfortunately. She's mad because I didn't want to loan her any money."

"Could be," I said noncommittally. I glanced around at all the professional equipment and the finished cupcakes on the table. "You've got quite a setup here."

"The shop does well. We make a lot on parties for kids."

"That's awesome," Cal piped up.

She threw him a shy smile.

Ask her out, Cal, I kept thinking as they gazed at each other. He glanced at me, and I tried to give him a look to nudge him along, but he didn't get it.

"One more thing," I said, then hesitated. "Have you ever had any drug or alcohol problems?"

She arched her eyebrows. "No, never. Why?"

"Just asking." I believed her. "I'm going to find your grandfather and see where that leads. And I'm following up on a few other things as well."

"I really appreciate it. I want this resolved." She started for the front and we followed. "Would you like some cupcakes?" she called over her shoulder.

"We couldn't," Cal said.

"My treat."

Now I *did* nudge Cal. Holly went behind the counter, and Sarah returned to the kitchen. Cal and I stood in front of the counter, and Holly waited for us to make our selections. He suddenly was speechless.

"What do you recommend?" I asked.

"The carrot cake cupcake is good, and I'm partial to the vanilla with raspberry filling."

Cal found his voice. "Either one."

"Both." She put them in a bag and handed it to him.

"Thank you," he murmured.

She turned to me. "And for you?" I selected vanilla raspberry and double chocolate, and then she said, "I'll put in a couple for your wife, if you think she'd enjoy them."

"She would, thanks." I smiled.

Another woman came into the shop, followed by two men in business-casual attire.

"We'll let you go," I said. "I'll be in touch as soon as I find out anything more."

Holly nodded. "Thanks." Then she was busy attending to her customers.

"Why didn't you ask her out?" I said to Cal when we hit the sidewalk.

"I just couldn't do it." He looked over his shoulder, then assessed himself. "Would she want to go out with me?"

"There were sparks there." Little ones.

He sighed. "Let's finish this case first, okay?"

"Sure."

We started for the parking garage, then I stopped.

"What're you doing after this?" I asked.

"I've got some work to do for this client tonight."

"Can we go somewhere and see what we can find out about Bob Morrow?"

"There's a Starbucks around the corner, and they'll have internet."

"Let's go," I said.

CHAPTER NINETEEN

"Hold on," Cal said. "I need to go get my laptop."

While he ran back to the parking garage, I went into the Starbucks, ordered us lattes, and found a table outside. Cal returned a few moments later with his backpack.

"How about we eat some of those cupcakes," he said as he pulled out his laptop.

I opened a plastic container that had his cupcakes in it. "Which one do you want?"

"I'll take the carrot cake," he said.

I handed him the cupcake. He took a bite, then set it aside and started typing on the computer.

"Wow! This is fantastic." He grabbed the cupcake again, wolfed down the rest of it in one big bite, and took a sip of his latte. "Boy, the latte doesn't live up to the cupcake."

I opened my container and grabbed a cupcake. I took a bite and nodded. "No kidding. This vanilla raspberry is incredible."

He started typing one-handed while he licked his fingers. "Let me see if I can find this guy Bob's credit cards."

He started humming and I watched as he worked. It only took me a couple of bites and my cupcake was gone, too.

"Willie is going to love these," I said as I picked up his container.

"Hey, that one's mine."

I ignored that. "What about that credit card info for Morrow?"

"It'll take me a few minutes," he said, then glanced over at me. "And don't think I didn't notice you deflecting the conversation from the cupcakes."

"You noticed that?"

He grinned. "I've got to find which credit cards Morrow had, and then I can see what he's been buying that might tell us something."

"Take your time," I said as I watched traffic go by on Washington Avenue. I sat for a few minutes, trying not to dive into the cupcake container.

Finally, Cal sat back in his chair. "Now this is interesting."

"What's that?" I asked.

"It looks like Morrow recently flew someplace."

I leaned forward. "Really?"

Cal glanced at me and smiled. "His credit card shows he booked a United flight."

"Where to?"

He shrugged. "Let me go to their website and get the details."

He focused on his laptop. I tapped my foot impatiently.

"He flew to Denver a week ago, on Friday," he announced a minute later. "And it looks like he's flying back to Dallas two days from now."

I did some quick math in my head. "That was four days before Shirley was murdered. Does this credit card show if he got a hotel in town?"

"Hang on, let me check."

He typed again, and I waited impatiently again.

"Here it is. He's staying at the Embassy Suites by Denver International Airport."

"Is that the one off Peña Boulevard?"

He nodded, and typed for a few seconds. "You get there from East Fifty-sixth Avenue." He rattled off the address.

"Hold on," I said. "Let me put it in my phone."

I nodded at his laptop. "Is there a number for the hotel?"

"Yes." He told me that as well. "Anything else?"

"No." I grinned at him. "My, aren't we in a mood," I said as I pulled out my cell phone and dialed the number.

He tossed the empty cupcake wrapper at me. On the phone, a pleasant female voice answered.

"It's a great day at the Embassy Suites Hotel at Denver International Airport. How may I direct your call?"

That was a mouthful. "I need Bob Morrow's room, please."

"One moment, sir."

I heard the sound of fingers on the keyboard, just as I'd heard so many times when I talked to Cal. It didn't take this woman long to find Morrow's room.

"Let me connect you."

"Thank you," I said.

A small click sounded through the phone. I waited as it rang several times and then went to a generic voicemail. I ended the call.

Cal glanced up at me. "He's not there?"

I shook my head, then sat back and crossed my arms. "I need to find him."

"You're not going to leave a message?"

"And say what? That I wonder if he murdered his ex?"

"You think he came here to see Shirley?"

"I'd say that's a good bet."

Cal had been typing while I made the call, and he pointed at the screen.

"He rented a Dodge pickup. Here's the license plate number."

"Good work." I put that information in my phone, too.

"Morrow's cell phone carrier is AT&T. Let me see if I can find his phone records." It took a bit, but then he sat back with a satisfied look on his face. "I found a list of all his recent phone calls. And guess what?"

I stared at him. "He called Shirley Durocher."

"That's right."

"When?"

"A week ago Monday."

"That's the day Shirley was killed," I said. "I doubt that's a coincidence."

He held up a finger. "Hold on. I'm going to access his saved messages."

I waited until he turned the laptop around.

"Hit play," he said.

I used the mouse and hit the play button, and suddenly Shirley's voice came through the computer speakers.

"Listen, Bob. Stop harassing me, and don't come around again. You owe me, and you know it, for all the crap you did to us, so leave me alone."

Shirley's voice was tight and bitter. Cal and I looked at each other.

"That sounds like the woman we knew," I said.

"What do you think she meant?" he asked.

I shrugged. I glanced at my phone with the hotel address on it. "If I can find this guy Bob Morrow, I'll ask him." I pointed at the laptop. "Can you find his driver's license?"

"Of course. But why?"

"So I know what he looks like. Then I'll go to his hotel and wait for him."

Cal's face was still blank.

"Are you thinking about Holly?"

He shrugged.

"If I'm going to wait for him," I continued, "I need to know what he looks like."

Cal turned red. "Oh, right." He set to work and did his magic, and a minute later, he turned the laptop back to me again. "Here's what Morrow looks like," he said.

We both stared at the screen. Morrow had a tanned, leathery face with wrinkles around the corners of his eyes, bushy eyebrows, and a beard. His full head of iron gray hair was neatly combed, and his eyes had a humorous cast. According to the license, he was six feet tall and weighed 180 pounds.

"This was the man who tormented Shirley and Karen?" I mused.

"He doesn't look very threatening," Cal observed.

"Well, looks can be deceiving."

Cal snorted. I studied the license carefully and memorized his face.

"What else do you need?" Cal asked.

"I think that's it for now," I said. I finished my latte. "I'll go out to the hotel and see if I can find him there."

Cal started to put away his laptop, but I held up a hand.

"Hold on. Let's show that picture to Holly."

He nodded, then zipped up his backpack, and flung it over his shoulder.

"I'm not much of a coffee drinker," he said as we started back toward the cupcake shop. "But that cupcake was great."

"Agreed."

When we entered the cupcake shop, Holly was busy wiping

down one of the counters. Her eyebrows shot up when she saw us.

"What's going on?" The cloth kept moving across the glass. "I've got to keep going, some last-minute orders are being picked up soon."

"No problem," I said.

Cal came up to the counter, set his laptop down, and let her see the picture of Bob Morrow.

"Do you recognize him?" I asked. "It's your grandfather."

Now the rag stopped moving, and her jaw dropped. She stared at the screen for a second, then shook her head. "Wow, that's my grandfather."

"You haven't seen him around?" I went on. "Maybe watching the store?"

Her eyes went from the laptop to me. "You're worrying me."

I nodded. "I think he's in Denver."

"He doesn't look familiar." She couldn't take her eyes away from the laptop. "Huh, so that's what he looks like."

"I'll find him," I said, "and ask him a few questions. In the meantime, if you see him, let me know."

"I will, and you be sure to tell me what he says."

I agreed. Cal closed the laptop, and we left just as another customer arrived.

"Remember, you need to ask her out," I said as we walked to our cars.

"All right, all right," he growled. "I need a little time."

"Okay." I held up my hands. "When we wrap up this case."

"That's right."

"Be careful with Bob Morrow," he said as he got into his car. "It's possible he's a murderer."

I nodded.

Cal's little Honda puttered to life, and he drove slowly out of the parking garage. I waited until he turned onto the street,

154

then walked to my car, my mind on Holly. I believed her when she said she didn't recognize Bob Morrow. I also thought that her apprehension about him was justified. It didn't strike me as coincidence that he was in Denver right when he ex-wife had been murdered. And until I found out why he was in town, I was worrying as well.

CHAPTER TWENTY

Rush-hour had begun by the time I drove out of Golden, and it took me a long time to go east on Interstate 70 to Peña Boulevard. I turned north, then got onto East Fifty-sixth Avenue, and soon came to Tower Road. I was amazed at how many houses and office buildings there were now in this part of town. It seemed as if just a few short years ago, there had been little out here except fields and open prairie. But with Denver's new airport out here, plus rapid growth in recent years, even this area was being built up. As a jet roared overhead, I wondered how people who lived around here tolerated that.

I soon came to the Embassy Suites Hotel. I drove around the parking lot, searching for the Dodge truck that Bob Morrow had rented, but I didn't see any with the license plate that matched the number I'd written down. I finally parked on the west side of the building and went inside.

The lobby was spacious, filled with leather chairs and couches arranged in small groupings. I walked past those to a long counter where a woman was typing at a computer.

"I'm looking for Bob Morrow," I said with a smile. "I'm not sure of his room number."

"I'm afraid I can't give out that information," she said with an equally charming smile. "If you'd like to wait for him, you can certainly do so." She gestured with a hand toward one of the sitting areas.

It was worth a try, but it didn't surprise me that she wouldn't give out the room number.

"Thanks," I said.

I walked toward one of the couches, then glanced over my shoulder. The woman was busy at the computer again, oblivious to me. I walked away from her and toward a large atrium decorated with a rock waterfall, a bar fashioned in dark wood tones, and more seating. Balconies on the upper floors overlooked the atrium, and beyond the balcony railings, I could see doors to hotel rooms. I looked around at all those room doors, wondering how to figure out which one was Morrow's.

I sauntered around the atrium, and noticed multiple banks of elevators. There was also a back entrance to the hotel. I finally settled into a chair in the middle of the atrium where I could see all the elevators and both entrances. It would be my best shot at seeing Morrow, if and when he returned.

While I waited, I pulled out my phone and texted Willie to let her know that I didn't know when I'd be home, then put my phone away and settled in. The atrium grew busier as business types and other guests made their way to the bar or sat at the tables talking and discussing the day. I was just one more hotel guest waiting in the lobby. Finally, a man in jeans, plaid shirt, and tan cowboy hat strode down the hall from the front entrance into the atrium.

Bob Morrow.

He was a big fellow, meatier than I expected, with a hint of a gut protruding over a large silver belt buckle. I stood up and headed toward him, but right then he put a cell phone to his ear and started talking. I leaned against a pillar and watched him. He suddenly turned and headed back toward the entrance. I swore under my breath and was on his heels.

He walked out the hotel entrance and to a white Dodge truck. As he got in, I ran to my 4-Runner, hopped in, and when he drove out of the parking lot, I was on his tail. He reached Tower Road, went to Fifty-sixth Avenue, and was soon headed south on Peña Boulevard. Traffic was heavy, but I was able to follow him without trouble. I was pretty sure he had no idea I was behind him. He drove the speed limit, and I kept him in sight, thinking maybe he was headed downtown. I cranked some '80s music and hummed along to the Go-Gos. But Morrow soon turned onto Central Park Boulevard and drove into the shops at Northfield Stapleton, a newer open-air shopping center. He went to East Forty-sixth Avenue and Unita Street, parked in the lot, and strode into Jim 'N Nick's Bar-B-Q.

I found a parking place in the next row from his truck and waited until he went inside, then followed. When I entered the restaurant, he was walking toward a table in a bar area across from the entrance. He sat down across from a bald man in a business suit. The restaurant foyer was crowded, and I had no problem loitering near the entrance while I watched Morrow. A minute later, a waiter came up to his table, spoke to him, and left. Then Morrow opened up a menu. It appeared he was going to be staying a while. And he didn't notice as I took a seat at the bar where I could keep my eye on him.

"What'll you have?" A tall thin bartender asked me.

"A Coke."

I would've loved a Fat Tire, one of my favorite microbrews, but since I didn't know how much more driving I'd be doing, I

RENÉE PAWLISH

decided against it. The bartender brought my soda, and I nursed it while I watched Morrow. He and the man in the business suit kept up a lively conversation while they sipped drinks, and then ate hors d'oeuvres that the waiter brought. Finally, Morrow pulled some papers from his pocket, unfolded and smoothed them out on the table, and handed them to the man in the suit. He perused them, then folded them back up and put them in his suit pocket.

With that, it seemed their visit was finished, and Morrow stood up. He shook the other man's hand, pulled out his wallet and laid some bills on the table, then marched out of the restaurant. I didn't lose any time paying for my Coke, and I dashed outside. When the white truck left the parking lot, I was again on his tail.

"What was that all about?" I wondered out loud as I kept the truck in sight.

The truck headed back to the highway, where traffic was still heavy. I kept it in sight for a while, but suddenly the truck veered to the right and turned onto Colorado Boulevard. I had to wait for a little black sports car to whiz by on my right, then I cut off a Mazda as I headed for the exit ramp. I frantically looked for the truck, and didn't notice that traffic was slowing down. I had to slam on my brakes in order not to hit the car in front of me. Up ahead, the truck was turning left through a yellow light. I had at least six cars in front of me, waiting to turn at the next green light.

"No!" I pounded the steering wheel.

After what seemed like an eternity, the light finally turned green, and I was able to turn. But as I drove down Colorado Boulevard, it was obvious that I'd lost the white truck. I swore as I turned into the parking lot of a strip mall. I sat facing Colorado Boulevard and watched the street for a while, but no white truck. I debated going back to the Embassy Suites to wait for Morrow to return, but decided against it. I was tired and, more importantly, hungry. I'd deal with Morrow later. I gave up and drove home.

"Hey, babe," Willie said to me as I walked through the door.

"Hi, hon."

I reached down and picked up Humphrey, who had bounded up to me. I scratched behind his ears and he immediately started to purr. It made me feel better.

"I've got Parmesan chicken in the oven," Willie said, "and I'm just fixing a salad. Does that sound okay?"

"That sounds delicious."

I walked into the kitchen, where Willie was standing at the counter, cutting up a tomato. I leaned over her shoulder and kissed her cheek.

"I missed you today," I said.

"Me, too."

She turned and gave me a lingering kiss, then kissed Humphrey on the head. I was grateful to be the first in line.

"How about—"

The sound of the real Humphrey Bogart interrupted her. My phone.

"Hang on a second," I said. I pulled out my phone and glanced at it. "It's Ace. Let me get this." I went into the other room and answered.

"Hey, Reed." Ace's voice was filled with excitement.

"What's up?"

"So Deuce and I have still been talking to some of the neighbors, right?"

"Right," I said. Where was this going? The smell of Parmesan chicken filled the air, and my stomach growled. Right then, I just wanted to sit back, have a beer, and enjoy some time with Willie.

"Well, I finally got a chance to talk to Mr. Darmody down the street. And guess what he said?"

"What?" How long was this going to take?

"He said he thought he heard someone outside the night Shirley was murdered."

"Oh? What did he hear?"

"Something about ... um ... I was on my way to work, Reed, and I didn't have anything to write it down. I don't remember all of it, but something about the ornery old woman. I'm sorry. If you want, I can run over and ask him, and I'll write it down."

I could picture him turning red.

"No, that's okay. I appreciate the help, but I'll just go over and ask him. You did a great job."

"Thanks. Anytime you need us, Deuce and I are happy to help."

"I can always count on the two of you." I genuinely meant that.

He thanked me, and I ended the call.

"Hey," I called into the kitchen, "I need to pop over and talk to Mr. Darmody, okay?"

"Don't be too long," Willie called from the kitchen. "The chicken will be done in a few minutes."

"Don't worry, I'll be back fast. I'm starving."

I heard her laughing as I went out the door. I hurried down the stairs and walked over to Mr. Darmody's house. A light was on in the living room window, and I heard the sound of a TV. I rapped loudly on the door. A moment later, Mr. Darmody appeared.

"Hello Reed," he said. "How are you tonight?"

"I'm fine, thanks. Do you have time for a quick question or two?"

"Sure, we're just watching Wheel of Fortune."

I could hear Pat Sajak in the background.

"Ace said you heard something outside the night Shirley was killed," I said.

He nodded slowly. "That's right. I talked to the police about it."

"Do you mind telling me what you told them?"

He shrugged. "It was around midnight, maybe before." He looked past me, toward Shirley's house. "I'd gotten up to shut the window – it had been cracked open to let in a little cool air, but it had gotten too cold – and I heard voices outside, so I looked out the window. I saw someone walk out of her house, and then he said, 'You ornery old woman, you'll get what's coming to you.' Then he headed off down the street."

"How did you know it was a man?"

"By the sound of his voice. It was lower, so I assumed it was a man."

"And you heard it that clearly?"

"Noise carries well in the dark night."

I nodded in agreement. "Do you know who it was?"

He shook his head. "It was dark, and I didn't see him very well."

I thought about Mr. Morrow. "Was he a taller guy, and a bit stocky, with a cowboy hat?"

"No, that doesn't sound like him. Like I said, it was dark, and I didn't see much, but no hat."

I thought about something else. "Have you had anything stolen lately?"

"A laptop. It was a nice one. I left it in my car and it got swiped. Took the case with my initials on it, too. L.D. What's anyone going to do with that?"

"Okay," I said. "I'll let you get back to your TV show."

"Tell Willie we said hi."

"Will do."

I gave him a friendly wave and walked back to the condo. Willie was just taking the chicken out of the oven.

"Set the table, will you?"

"Sure."

I got out dishes and silverware, and while we ate, I told her the latest about my case. When I finished, she was most concerned about Cal.

"It's obvious he likes Holly," she said. "We need to help get them together."

"Oh, now you're a matchmaker like my mother."

She laughed, but her wrinkled brow told me she was plotting something. "Maybe we could have Cal and Holly over for dinner. Or we could go on a double date. Then we can get the two of them talking."

I thought about what Cal had said. "Let's finish this case first."

"Yes, right." She nodded halfheartedly as she stared at the table, thinking. She was still figuring out her plan.

And I was mulling over my own plans. I really wanted to talk to Bob Morrow, but I couldn't see any way to do that unless I went back to the hotel and waited for him to return. If he was already back in his room, I'd be wasting my time. But if he wasn't, I could talk to him when I saw him. Which could be a long time. I sighed.

Willie looked up. "What?"

"I need to go back to Bob Morrow's hotel and wait for him." I explained what I'd been thinking. "It could be a long night, and I'm not looking forward to that."

She got up, took her dishes to the sink, then came over and kissed me. "The life of a PI."

"Such sympathy."

She kissed me harder. Then, in her sultriest femme fatale whisper: "I'll be waiting for you to get back."

I eyed her up and down. "Waiting?"

"I promise." She giggled and walked out of the room.

I stood up, tempted to follow her. But duty called, so I quickly cleared the dishes, then grabbed my keys, and my Glock from a locked box in the bedroom closet, and headed out the door.

CHAPTER TWENTY-ONE

The moon fell behind some clouds as I walked to my car. I got in, flipped a U-turn, and headed up the street and onto the next block, my mind on Bob Morrow. Then I suddenly hit the brakes and craned around in my seat. I'd just passed a white pickup. I backed up until I was parallel with it. No one was inside.

Could it be?

I backed up a little more until I could see the rear license plate.

"Well, what do you know?" I said to no one.

It was Morrow's rented truck. I glanced all around, searching for him. Where was he? A chill ran down my arms. Was he watching me right now? I continued up the street, my eyes scanning left and right, but I didn't see him. But then, I'm not sure I expected to. I had a pretty good idea where he would be.

I drove to the next block, found a parking space, and pulled in. I shut off the 4-Runner, then sat in the dark for a minute. The street was momentarily quiet, no cars or people around. I quietly eased out of the car and shut the door. I listened. Only the sound of traffic on the surrounding streets. I hurried to the end of the block, crossed the street, and pressed myself against the back fence of the house on the corner. Then I peered down the alley that ran behind our building and Shirley Durocher's house. I couldn't see anything in the darkness.

A few blocks away, a car turned, its headlights coming toward me. I ducked around the corner of the fence so I wouldn't be spotted and tiptoed down the alley. I couldn't see very well, so I stepped carefully. Near another fence, a dog started barking. I jumped and then sped up, praying I wouldn't stumble as I ran, until I reached the back of our building. Then I stopped to catch my breath. Once I was breathing normally again, I listened.

Silence.

I continued down the alley until I reached a dumpster near the rear of Shirley's house. I crouched down near it and studied her back yard. I didn't see anyone.

I stared at her house. Light streamed out of the kitchen window, and a minute later, Holly Durocher passed by. I hadn't recalled her saying she'd be there, and I wondered what she was doing: going through more stuff? Had something we talked about prompted her to drop by?

I stayed down until my knees began to hurt from crouching so long, then stood up and stretched my legs. On the street, a car went by, and a different dog began barking. Then more silence.

After a few more minutes, I moved closer to the house, where I could see along one side. Through another window, I spotted Holly again. I sneaked to the corner of Shirley's yard, knelt down by a chain-link fence, and waited. I was sure Bob Morrow was around, but where? I listened, and again heard only traffic sounds. I had on a light jacket, and after a while, the chill of the night air seeped through the thin fabric. I ignored that and continued to wait. The moon finally emerged from the clouds and provided a glimmer of light. Periodically I saw Holly through the windows, and I wondered how long she would be there.

Maybe I'd been wrong about Morrow, I thought. If he had been around, perhaps he'd left while I was sneaking down the alley.

I stood up and was about to go into the back yard when I saw movement in some bushes near the side window. I froze and watched that spot in the silvery gloom. The shadow moved again. A man was hunkered down by the side of the house, watching the window. It had to be Morrow. I stayed where I was and watched that spot.

What exactly did he want? I wondered. *Would he try to hurt Holly?*

On the one hand, I was tempted to confront the man now, but on the other hand, I wanted to see what he would do. I slowly crouched down, keeping my eye on the shadow and the windows.

Holly worked for a while longer. I lost track of the time, but I couldn't risk looking at my watch. Then the lights in the house went off, and I heard the front door open and shut. I could see down the side of the house to the street. Seconds later, a figure appeared under a streetlight near Shirley's house. Holly carried a box in her arms, and she set it down while she dug keys from her pocket. The shadow in the bushes shifted and he craned to get a better view of Holly. I braced myself, wondering what he would do. But the figure stayed still as Holly unlocked her car, grabbed the box, and put it in the back seat. Then she walked around the car, got in the driver's side, and drove off.

The shadow stood up, and I got a better glimpse of him. Unless I missed my guess, it was Bob Morrow. He glanced toward the street, and then to the back of the house. I didn't move a muscle and held my breath. He kept looking in my direction, and I wondered if he'd seen me, but then he tiptoed quietly toward the back yard. He reached the gate, eased up the latch, and let himself into the yard. He listened for a moment, then hurried over to the back porch and up to the door. He glanced around again and tried the doorknob. I didn't think Holly was stupid enough to leave the house unlocked, and I was right. Sounds of the doorknob rattling filled the air, then stopped.

Morrow turned and peered into the yard. Satisfied no one had heard him, he sneaked quietly up to a window by the door and tried it, but it was locked. He went back around the side of the house and pushed at a window. A loud creak ripped into the darkness. I mentally groaned. Holly had thought to lock the doors, but she hadn't checked all the windows.

Morrow paused and listened, then pushed on the window. He quickly got it open, then hefted himself up onto the sill, his grunts carrying across the stillness. He got his torso through the window and wiggled inside. Finally, just his legs stuck out. Then they vanished.

I hopped over the fence, stopped its rattling with my hand, and waited to see if Morrow had heard. Nothing happened, so I dashed through the yard. I reached the corner of the house and pressed myself against it. The side window was a few feet away. Inside, something thumped. I waited, but it stayed quiet. Then the back doorknob rattled and the door opened. I ducked down and looked toward the porch, waiting for Morrow to appear. He didn't.

I eased myself up to the kitchen window and peeked inside. Morrow was standing on the other side of the room, a flashlight in his hand. He was looking at some papers on the kitchen

THE DAMNED DON'T DIE

table, oblivious to my presence. I thought about the back door and the side window.

He must've left the door open, I thought, *in order to leave himself a quick escape if he needed it.*

I ducked under the window, then stood up and headed for the door. He wasn't going to slip through my fingers this time.

CHAPTER TWENTY-TWO

When I got to the door, I pulled my Glock from my ankle holster and held it up. Then I carefully turned the doorknob and pushed on the door. It opened quietly, and I stepped inside the kitchen. Morrow was still at the table, looking at the papers. I took a step into the room and raised the gun.

"Turn around real slow, and put your hands where I can see them," I said in a low tone.

Morrow whirled around and dropped the flashlight. It clattered to the floor with a loud thump.

"Who are you?" His voice warbled.

"Hands in the air," I said.

He raised his hands slowly. The flashlight shone on the wall between us, and it bathed the room in an eerie glow.

"Back up," I ordered him.

He took a step back and started to lower his hands.

"Unh-uh," I said. "Hands up."

His hands shot back into the air. I took a quick step forward, bent down and grabbed the flashlight, then straightened up. I shuffled backwards, the gun still on him. I put the flashlight on him, and he blinked at the sudden light.

"Who are you?" He asked again.

I glanced around. "What are you looking for?"

"My money."

I pointed for him to sit in one of the chairs. "Keep your hands where I can see them."

He stepped over to a kitchen chair and sat down, then put his hands on his thighs, palms down.

"You going to answer my question?" He spoke with a deep Texas drawl. He eyed me warily.

"Your granddaughter hired me."

His jaw fell open. "My ... granddaughter?"

I nodded. "Holly."

He stared at me for a minute as he put things together. "My granddaughter? How is she?"

"She's doing all right, except for the fact that the police think she might've murdered her grandmother."

"Shirley?" He shook his head. "I can't believe Holly would do that."

"How do you know?"

He shrugged. "I guess I don't know, but I just can't believe anyone would kill their own flesh and blood."

"It happens plenty, but in this case, I tend to agree with you."

He studied me for a moment. "If Holly hired you, are you a private investigator?"

I nodded. "That's right. You want to tell me what you're looking for?"

"I told you, my money. Shirley owes me a boatload."

"From what I heard, you scammed a lot of money out of Shirley. That's why she left you, right?"

"Are you kidding me?" he snapped. "I don't know what you

heard, but Shirley took all of our money and ran. She left me without a cent. I couldn't even pay the mortgage that month."

I leaned back against the counter, but kept the gun trained on him. "I'm listening. Enlighten me."

He scratched his head, let out a sigh, and put his hand back on his thigh. "Boy, that was a long time ago. Talk about dredging up bad memories." He looked away from the flashlight beam. "Me and Shirley got together too young, we didn't know what we were doing."

"Durocher is Shirley's maiden name, right?"

He nodded. "She didn't want to take my name. Anyway, things were all right at first, but that woman, boy, she knew how to be cantankerous. We had Karen, and even then, Shirley was mean. We'd been fighting, and I was out of town when she had the baby, so she didn't even tell them who the father was."

"I'll bet that hurt."

He nodded. "I tried to make it work. But nothing seemed good enough for Shirley, and when Karen was still a baby, she left me. I was working in the oil fields at the time, and I came home for the weekend, and they were gone. Shirley'd cleared out all the money from the bank and from some hiding places we had in the house. I tried to hunt her down, but I didn't know where she went, and her family wouldn't tell me. I think they didn't like me because of things she told them, but it wasn't true." He waved a hand in the air. "I know I wasn't the perfect husband, I probably drank too much and that kind of thing, but it wasn't all me. She took my daughter from me, too." He got a faraway look in his eyes, as if thinking about what he'd lost. "And my granddaughter."

"Did you ever hit Shirley or Karen?"

He shook his head vehemently. "No way."

I contemplated him for a minute. "And after all this time,

you come back to Denver, saying Shirley owes you money. And it just happens to be right around the time she was murdered."

He nodded. "I tried to talk to her, but she wouldn't listen. And then," he hesitated, "she was killed."

"Were you watching the house?"

"Yes. You saw me the other day."

I crossed my arms. "And I'm supposed to believe you had nothing to do with Shirley's murder?"

"That's right," he said firmly.

"You've had years to try to get the money back from her, so again, why come back now?"

"I wasn't just trying to get the money she took back then, I wanted to get back the money that she's been taking from me all these years."

I was surprised by that. "What?"

"You heard me right. Shirley's been taking me to the cleaners for years."

"How so?"

"That's a story in itself." He snorted. "I heard she went to Dallas and hooked up with a guy there. For all I know, she might've left me for him. She dumped him – I think there was some kind of trouble, gambling maybe. She was in with the wrong crowd, from what I understand, and she was lucky to be alive. But then, the damned don't die, do they? They just make everyone else's lives miserable.

"Anyway, she finally contacted me. Well, a lawyer contacted me, and said I owed alimony. I didn't have the money to fight it, so I agreed to pay her. And I've been paying her alimony for years. But," he jabbed a finger at me, "I just found out a few months ago she'd gotten married again. You know what that means?"

"Once she remarried, you didn't have to pay her alimony anymore."

"You got that right. But I've been paying her, every single month, for years."

I thought for a second. "But I researched her. How come that second marriage didn't come up?"

He shrugged. "I only found out because I ran into her brother recently and he finally told me. It slipped out, is more like it. Shirley and that guy went to some small town outside Vegas, and it was a quick thing. It was a long time ago, and records weren't as good as they are now. And I was never looking to see if she'd remarried."

"Huh."

A dog barked, and he jumped. I glanced out the kitchen window, thinking I'd seen movement. I kept the Glock on Morrow, but went over to the door and looked out.

Nothing.

I turned back to Morrow. "Go on."

"Once her brother told me about the marriage, I did some more digging. I hired a private investigator myself, and he went to that town. It took him a while to unearth the license, so don't feel bad you missed it. Anyway, I've been paying her cash all this time, and I didn't have to."

"I looked through Shirley's bank records as well. Why didn't I see deposits from you?"

"I just told you, I've been paying her cash."

"Cash? You've been sending cash through the mail all this time?"

"Yep. That's what she insisted on, and so I did it. When I tried to send checks, she got furious with me and wouldn't cash them. So I did what she said. It was easier that way."

"Did you send Shirley notes when you sent her the money?"

He nodded. "Sometimes. Just trying to be friendly, even if I didn't like her. I hoped she'd let me see Karen. I even asked about it."

I'd not seen any of those letters. "But in one of them, you threatened her."

"No, I didn't."

"You said something about wanting to talk to her, and that you were tired of what she was doing to you, and that it ends now. That sounds like a threat to me."

"That wasn't from me. Honest."

"Come with me." I gestured for him to follow me. "Watch yourself." I held up the gun.

We went into the living room, and I eyed him as I moved over to the desk.

I looked around for the note that Holly had shown me, hoping she'd returned it this evening. It wasn't there. I turned back to him, then indicated we should go back in the kitchen. He sat back down, and I kept my distance.

"I didn't say anything like that," he insisted.

I wasn't sure I believed him, but I went on. "Once you found out about Shirley's second marriage, you came up here to talk to her. Let me guess, she told you to take a hike."

He nodded. "That's right. She was shocked to see me, but she denied the other marriage, and said she was entitled to all the money I'd been giving her, that I'd agreed to pay her alimony. So I met with the son of a friend of mine. He's a lawyer here in town. He's doing this as a favor to me, because I don't have a lot of money. We were going to take Shirley to court, and then, well, she's dead. We're not sure what to do now."

"Is that who you met at Jim 'N Nick's Bar-B-Q?"

He raised his eyebrows. "You've been following me?"

"Of course." I gestured around the room. "What were you looking for?"

"Anything that might help me prove that Shirley had remarried. Or anything that might help me get my money back."

"Have you broken in before?"

"No." He held up a hand. "That's the truth."

I probably shouldn't have, but I believed him.

"What were you doing a week ago, Monday night?" I asked.

"The night she was murdered? It just so happens I was in Cheyenne."

I thought about the snooping Cal had done on Morrow's credit cards. Cal hadn't seen any hotel rentals from there.

"I was with a friend in Cheyenne," Morrow said, as if he'd known what I was thinking. "I drove up that evening and had dinner and drinks with him, bought gas around one in the morning, and then decided I should stay the night with him. My friend will verify that."

"Call him."

"Now?"

I nodded. "Take out your phone, carefully."

He did as I said, then made the call. He put the phone on speaker and set it on the table. A sleepy male voice answered a moment later.

"Hey, Bob. What's up? Is everything all right?"

"Hi, Joe. Yes, it's all good. One thing, real quick. When I came up to visit, how long was I with you?"

"What kind of question is that?"

"Please, just answer."

"You stayed all night." The voice sounded bemused. "A little too much to drink at dinner, remember? You stopped for gas and then called me and said you didn't think you should drive all the way back to Denver. Is your wife giving you a hard time?"

"Something like that."

He laughed. "Well, tell her you were in good hands."

"Will do."

Morrow ended the call and looked at me. "Satisfied?"

I had to admit, it didn't sound like either one was lying.

"Hold on," I said. I pulled out my phone and called Cal.

"One thing," I said quickly when he answered. "Did Morrow buy gas in Cheyenne the night Shirley was murdered?"

"Let me check."

My tone was all business, so he didn't joke around. He typed for a moment. Morrow stared at me as we waited.

"Yes," Cal finally said. "Around one in the morning."

There was no way Morrow could've murdered Shirley sometime after midnight in Denver and been in Cheyenne around the same time. I thanked Cal, told him I'd call him later, and ended the call.

"I know you think I murdered Shirley," he said, "but I didn't, and I couldn't have. I just wanted my money back, and to stop paying her alimony."

I thought for a second. "Why'd you just watch Holly in the window? Why didn't you come in and talk to her?"

"That was Holly?" he asked. "I didn't even know what she looked like." His voice choked, and he cleared his throat. "Are you going to call the police on me?"

"Breaking and entering."

"So were you."

I jerked a thumb at the door. "It was open, so technically, I didn't break in."

"Neither one of us should be here," he said.

"Point taken."

"How long have you been watching the house?"

"Just a few times."

I thought about the light I'd seen on in the house after Holly had said she'd left. "Were you here the other night?"

He looked away, then nodded. "Just for a minute. I finally got the nerve to get inside and look around, but I didn't stay." He put a hand on his chest. "I'm not a thief. I thought I was going to have a heart attack when I came through the window."

"But you came back."

"I needed to see if I could find anything helpful."

I stepped back over to the counter. "You should go now. And don't come back here. If you want information, get it from Holly. I'm sure she'll want to get to the bottom of your alimony situation as much as you do."

"Will she talk to me?"

"I'll ask her and call you."

"Let me give you my number."

"I already have it."

"You–" He grunted. "Right, the private eye. None of my information is safe with you around."

I didn't say anything to that.

"May I get up?"

I nodded. "Empty your pockets."

"I didn't take anything," he said as he complied.

He showed me his wallet, some change, and his car keys. He didn't have anything else.

"I'll be in touch," I said.

He moved cautiously to the kitchen door, opened it, and left. He passed by the window, and I darted into the other room, where I watched him walk to the sidewalk. He glanced back at the house, then started off down the street. I ran to the living room and stepped onto the front porch and watched down the street. Morrow was in front of my building, walking fast. A minute later, red taillights came on, and the white truck pulled into the street and drove off in the other direction.

I hurried back inside, checked the front door to make sure it was locked, then locked all the windows. I went into the kitchen and looked around one final time, then let myself out the back door, making sure it was locked as well. I trotted across the yard to the fence, slipped out through the gate, and headed back down the alley. I retrieved my car and parked in front of my building. When I went upstairs, Willie was sitting at the table, working on her laptop. Humphrey was curled up contentedly sleeping on her lap. Was it possible to be jealous of a kitten?

"Did you find that guy Morrow?"

I nodded and told her what had happened. "If Morrow didn't have anything to do with Shirley's murder, I'm back to square one."

She petted Humphrey's head. "You have other suspects, right?"

"Yeah, and I'll have to keep looking into it, but it can wait until tomorrow." I grinned at her. "I think you promised me something for later."

She closed her laptop and set Humphrey on the floor.

"Your time's up," I said as I scratched his head.

He scampered off as she stood up. She cocked a finger at me to follow her into the bedroom.

Her promise was indeed good.

CHAPTER TWENTY-THREE

The next morning, I slept later than I meant to. I finally show-ered, dressed, and went into my office. I called Holly at the cupcake shop, and she answered sounding a bit harried.

"Hey, Reed, this isn't the best time."

"I'll keep it quick," I said. "You were at the house last night."

She hesitated. "That's right. Were you watching me?"

"Actually I was watching somebody *else* watch you."

"Who?"

"Your grandfather."

It took her a long time to respond. "My grandfather? You're kidding. What was he doing at Grandmother's house?"

I explained what had happened last night, and that Morrow wanted to meet Holly.

"Wow. I don't know what to say. You don't think he had anything to do with my grandmother's death?"

"I don't think so. His alibi checked out. Why don't I give you his number, and you can call him if and when you're comfortable."

"Uh, okay let's do that."

I gave her Morrow's number. "One more quick thing. Have you noticed anything missing from your grandmother's house?"

"I haven't been able to find a couple of necklaces that Grandmother sometimes wore."

"What did they look like?"

"One was an opal pendant with some small diamonds, and the other was a ruby on a gold chain. She kept them in little blue jewelry boxes. Don't ask me why I remember that, but I do."

She had just described the empty blue jewelry boxes I'd seen in Phil Epstein's underwear drawer. It seemed that maybe I'd found the neighborhood thief.

"Did someone steal them?" Holly asked.

"Possibly. Oh, one more thing. Do you still have the note that was in the envelope you showed me?

"Yes, I have it with me."

"Will you be at the house later tonight?"

"I'm not sure. Why?"

"I'd like to see that note again."

I told her I still needed to follow up on some other things, and that I'd update her again as soon as I had any new information. Just as I ended the call, my phone rang. It was Cal.

"What's up, O Great Detective?" he greeted me. He seemed in a better mood this morning. "Based on the call from you last night, I take it you found Morrow?"

I slapped my forehead. "I forgot to call you."

"It's okay. But I am curious about what happened."

I told him about my encounter with Morrow. "I believe him."

"So that means you're back to square one."

"Maybe. Although I think Phil Epstein has been stealing

things, so I'm going to check into that. Maybe he's also a murderer."

"Okay, let me know if you need anything else. We need to find Shirley's murderer."

"We?"

"I said I'd help Holly. Don't make anything of it."

"Okay, no problem."

I ended that call, but immediately called Phil Epstein's office. When I asked for him, the receptionist hesitated.

"He's not in right now. Can I put you through to his voice mail?"

"Are you expecting him today?"

"I ... Mr. Epstein has taken a temporary leave of absence. I can connect you to the person who's covering for him, if you'd like."

"Where is Epstein?"

"I'm afraid I'm not at liberty to say."

I ended the call without bothering to leave a message. Then I called Spillman.

"What's up, Ferguson?" she asked after I identified myself.

"You might look into a guy named Bob Morrow." I explained who he was and what I'd found out. "I don't think he murdered Shirley Durocher, but you might find something I didn't."

"Good work."

I told her what else I'd found out, ending with, "I'm going to look for Phil Epstein now."

"Why?"

I told her what I could, again leaving out that I'd searched his condo. "I don't like that he seems to be missing."

She sighed. "Me, either. I'll put out an APB on him."

I didn't know if an all-points bulletin would help. "Let me know if you find him."

"Will do." She thanked me and ended the call.

I got my Glock and went out into the kitchen. Willie was sitting at the table, the laptop open in front of her, but Humphrey had her attention.

"He is just so darn cute," she said. She held him up. "Look at that face."

"I have to admit, he *is* adorable. Hey, I've got to go."

She looked up at me and smiled. "Go catch the bad guys. I've got a lot to do around here, but if you can make it home for dinner, let me know, okay?"

"You bet."

I kissed her, then grabbed my keys, and headed out the door. I walked to Phil Epstein's building and let myself in the foyer. I had to again wait until someone came out so I could get in, then I headed up to the third floor. As I walked down the hall, I was surprised to see a woman with long brown hair standing by his door. As I approached, she turned and looked at me, her eyes wide, a mix of surprise and concern.

"Um, hello." Her voice was soft. "Are you looking for Phil?"

I nodded, and explained who I was. "Is he home?"

She shook her head. "I don't think so. He was supposed to have the kids last night, but he never showed up. I called him several times, but he hasn't answered." She stared at the door. "It's not like him. Frankly, I'm getting concerned."

"You're his ex-wife?"

"Laura."

"When you last saw Phil, was he acting suspicious? Was there anything that made you think something was wrong?"

"No. He may have been a little stressed out lately, but I don't think I would say that it was concerning. Do you think I should call the police?"

"It's not a bad idea," I said. "I'll see what I can find out as well."

THE DAMNED DON'T DIE

She ran a hand through her hair, then looked at me. "I just don't understand." Her voice trailed off.

"Do you mind if I ask you a few questions?"

"If it will help find Phil, absolutely. We may be divorced, but I don't want to see anything bad happen to him."

"Have you had any issues with him since you got divorced? You said that it's not like him not to contact you, but any problems with him paying your alimony or child support, things like that?"

"No, he's been really good about that. I know that money is tight for him, but he's always managed to get it paid, and I appreciate it."

I thought for a second. "Has he been depressed, or does he have drinking or gambling problems?"

"No, nothing like that. Phil's a good guy, we just weren't good together."

"Did Phil ever mention Shirley Durocher?"

She nodded. "Yes, I've heard that name."

"Did Phil have any issues with her that he shared with you?"

"No, just that he didn't like her." Her brow furrowed. "For instance, I dropped the kids off one night and he had just gotten off the phone with her. He was pretty angry. I asked him about it, and he mentioned her name, and said that she was a pain in the butt. That's it."

I couldn't think of anything else to ask her right then, so I pulled a business card from my wallet and handed it to her.

"If you see or hear from Phil, will you let me know?"

"Absolutely, and you do the same."

She pulled a pad and pen from her purse, and wrote down her name and number. I recognized her name now. I'd seen her name on the envelopes in Phil's condo.

We walked down the stairs and outside together. I waited to leave until she got into her car and drove off. Then I ran to the

4-Runner, grabbed the lock-pick set that I keep behind the driver's seat, and hurried back to Epstein's building. I waited until someone came out, then dashed inside. I went up to the third floor again and used the lock-pick set on his door. In moments, I was in his condo.

I quickly looked around. The place was exactly as I'd remembered it. It didn't look as if Epstein had been there since I had. I went into the bedroom, looked in the dresser, and saw the blue jewelry boxes Holly had described to me. I took a picture of them and of some other jewelry I found hidden under a stack of tee shirts. I'd show the pictures to Holly later, and see if she knew whether the pieces belonged to Shirley as well.

When I finished, I looked around a little more carefully. On the nightstand was a laptop case with the initials "L.D." on it. Mr. Darmody's, no doubt. Epstein was definitely a thief, but had he stolen something even more valuable from Shirley, something he'd commit murder for?

I needed to find out. I quietly let myself out of his condo, hurried downstairs, and headed for the 4-Runner. I didn't know where Epstein was, but there was one place I could start looking.

CHAPTER TWENTY-FOUR

I stopped for a quick bite at a Burger King, then drove to Twenty-sixth and Emerson. I parked down the street from the four-story apartment building that Phil Epstein had visited the day before yesterday. A few people were sitting on their balconies, and a woman was playing with her kids in the front yard of the house down the block, but otherwise it was quiet. I was able to see the third-floor apartment I'd watched before, but from a distance I couldn't tell whether anyone was home. I checked my Glock in my ankle holster, then got out, locked the 4-Runner, and headed to the apartment building. The metal staircase clinked loudly as I walked up to the third floor.

I went down the walkway to the apartment I'd seen Epstein visit – 304 – then rapped loudly on the door. Inside, I could hear the crashing sounds of heavy metal music. I knocked again, heard cursing, and then the door opened. A thin, wiry guy with slicked-back black hair and a crooked nose stared at me. The music was even louder now.

"Whaddaya want?" His beady eyes narrowed.

He didn't look particularly threatening, but when I glanced

behind him, I saw a gun sitting on a beat-up coffee table. I was suddenly more wary. I had no idea what his name was or anything about him, so I winged it.

"Are you McKane?" I asked.

"Who wants to know?"

"I–" That's as far as I got.

"Get the hell out of here." He started to close the door.

I put a hand out to stop him and said, "Hey, I'm looking for Phil Epstein. Do you know him? I think he came around here the other day."

"Who?"

"Phil Epstein. You know him. He's got long black hair and kind of a flat face. I know he visited you, the day before yesterday."

"I don't know what you're talking about."

He glanced around, but didn't make eye contact. He wasn't a very good liar.

I shifted and looked past him into the apartment. There was a ratty couch opposite the door, and a TV sitting on a little entertainment center. Several laptops, tablets, boxes, and other electronic equipment was on a coffee table.

"What kind of operation are you running here?" I asked.

He tried to fill the doorway to block my view, but he was too thin to make much difference. The tough act wasn't really working. But there was the gun ...

"I don't know who you are, but–" he snarled.

"I'm the law."

I pulled out my wallet and quickly flashed my PI license. He couldn't tell I wasn't actually with the police. His eyes widened, and he licked his lips.

"I'm not doing anything wrong," he said.

"I just want to know where Phil Epstein is."

"I told you, I don't know."

I pointed behind him. "Mind if I look around?"

"He's not here, and unless you got a warrant, I got nothing else to say to you."

With that, he quickly slammed the door. I stood there for a minute. That was a bust, but then, I didn't really expect that he would tell me anything. I still had to try. Just then the music died, and I heard his voice.

"Hey, man, we got a problem. A cop's looking for Epstein. We got to get him before—" his voice faded away, and I didn't hear anything else.

I'd spooked him. That was good. I turned away from the door and headed for the stairs. I went down to the first floor and hunted around until I found the manager's unit. I knocked on the door, and a middle-aged man with thinning hair opened it.

"Yes?" His voice was low and gravelly. The smell of cigarette smoke drifted out to me.

I got right to the point. "The thin guy in 304. What's his full name?"

"Is there a problem? I don't normally give out that information."

Once again, I pulled out my PI license and flashed it quickly. It worked like a charm.

"Donald McKane, but he goes by Donnie. Look, I don't want any trouble around here, okay?"

"I'm not trying to cause any trouble," I said. "I just needed the name. Thanks for your time."

I whirled around and left before he could ask more questions. I went back to the 4-Runner and looked up Donald McKane on the Internet. It took a little bit of searching, but I stumbled upon a website that gave his criminal history. He'd been in jail a few times and had served a year in prison for burglary. I glanced back up at the apartment building.

What a charming guy, I thought. *And what was Phil Epstein doing with him?*

McKane also had a Facebook page, where he mostly posted about partying and sports. If he was into illegal activity, which I suspected he was, at least he was smart enough not to put it out on the Internet.

I sat back and watched the apartment building. If I'd heard McKane correctly, he knew where Epstein was. I didn't know how long it would take before McKane would leave, but my guess was that he would, and I hoped he'd lead me to Epstein.

However, the afternoon dragged on, and McKane never appeared. I listened to music, read an ebook on my phone, and grew bored. The street grew busier as kids came home from school, and people began returning from work. I kept waiting for someone to ask me what I was doing there, but no one did. Shadows crept across the street, and I pulled out my phone and called Willie.

"Hey, babe, how's it going?" she asked.

"Not too bad, but I don't know when I'll be home. I'm on the track of Phil Epstein now."

"Oh, okay. You think you'll be back for dinner?"

"I doubt it, but I'll call you if things change."

"Would you care if I just went to dinner with Darcy?"

"Sure, why don't you do that," I said. "I'll grab something when I can."

"Sounds good. And babe, be careful."

"I will."

I put my phone away and continued to watch the building. Just as dusk fell, the door to 304 opened, and Donnie McKane came out. He closed the door, pulled on the knob to make sure it was locked, and walked downstairs. I scrunched down in my seat so he wouldn't see me. He reached the sidewalk, looked around, then walked down the block. He got into an older model Mustang, and the engine fired to life. Then the Mustang pulled into the street and drove away.

I waited until he got to the next block and then followed him, but I didn't turn on my headlights. The Mustang turned the corner and went east on Twenty-sixth. We reached Colorado Boulevard, and McKane went north. Traffic was heavy, but that didn't stop him from driving crazily. I wondered if he thought he was being followed, so I was careful to keep plenty of cars between us, and I almost lost him more than once.

McKane stayed on Colorado and crossed Interstate 70, then turned on Forty-eighth Avenue. We were in an industrial part of town full of warehouses. I thought McKane might turn into one of them, but he eventually stopped in front of a junkyard. Lots of cars in various stages of disrepair filled the lot. I braked at the corner and watched as McKane got out of his car. He unlocked a gate and drove through.

I parked and watched the car. It drove past a little trailer that had a streetlight above a door with a sign that read "Office." Then I lost sight of the car. I hopped out of the 4-Runner and ran down the block, keeping low, thankful that darkness had fallen. A six-foot-high chain-link fence surrounded the junkyard. I peered through it, searching for McKane. Then I saw him toward the back of the lot. He was approaching a large metal storage locker.

I backtracked and went along the other side of the lot, and as I reached the back of the lot, I sneaked along the perimeter fence carefully. The sound of the storage door being opened carried over the fence. Then I heard McKane's voice.

"You lied when you said no one was suspicious of you." McKane's voice was menacing.

"What are you talking about?"

It was Phil Epstein, and his voice warbled with fear.

"Cop came around today, looking for you."

"I don't know anything about that. If you let me go, I'll get you your money, okay?" Epstein said desperately.

A cracking sound came from the storage locker, and Epstein yelped. McKane must've smacked Epstein.

"If you're lying to me—" McKane didn't finish the sentence.

"I'm not! Listen, I am not doing any good in here. If you let me go, I'll get your money. I promise."

"Yeah? I'll be back with Davey in a little bit, and then we'll deal with you."

"Wait! Don't leave."

The rest of what Epstein said was drowned out by McKane's swearing. He came out of the storage locker and closed the door. I noticed, however, that he didn't lock it. He then headed back through the lot to his car. I ducked down as his headlights cut through the darkness, and waited until the Mustang reached the street. McKane got out and locked the gate, then hopped back in his car and drove away. I didn't have much time. I stood up and listened.

Lots of traffic noise, but nothing coming from the junkyard. I was concerned that there might be a guard dog in the lot, and wouldn't that have been just my luck. I found a rock on the ground and threw it over the fence. It hit one of the old clunkers with a loud thunk. I waited to see if it attracted any attention. No one came out of the office, and no dogs barked. I threw one more rock, just for good measure, but nothing happened.

I decided I was in the clear and made my move. I climbed to the top of the fence as quietly as I could, then dropped to the ground on the other side. I stole over to the storage locker, lifted the latch, and opened the door.

"Phil?" I whispered.

A muffled sound came from the back of the storage locker. I

pushed the door open wider, trying to let any bit of light in. It was of little help. I felt my way to the back of the unit, then saw a dark form in the corner.

"Phil?"

He nodded frantically. I reached down and took a gag out of his mouth.

"Thank God you're here." His voice was raspy. "Get me out of here, please!"

"I'm working on it," I said.

His hands and feet were tied, and I worked to loosen the knots as quickly as I could.

"Hurry!" he said.

"I am."

I finally got the knots free and helped Epstein to his feet.

"I can hardly stand," he whispered. "I don't know if I can walk."

He didn't have shoes on, and that wasn't going to help our situation.

"You're going to have to try," I said. "You have to climb the fence."

"Climb a fence?"

"Yes, that's the only way out of here."

He grunted as we moved to the other end of the storage locker. I started to close the door, but then saw headlights on the street.

"Move," I hissed at Epstein.

He was having trouble walking, so I didn't bother latching the door, but hurried to him. I helped him, and we made our way as fast as we could to the fence. His legs seemed to loosen up the more he walked, and he was able to make it over the fence without too much difficulty. Then we did an ungraceful walk-run toward my car. That's when I noticed the Mustang parked in front of the junkyard entrance.

CHAPTER TWENTY-FIVE

"Be quiet," I murmured.

We heard the sounds of the gate opening as I helped Epstein into the passenger seat, then got in and started the car. I glanced in the rearview mirror and groaned. The Mustang was backing up, headed toward us.

"Get down!" I said to Epstein.

We ducked down and the Mustang passed by. I sat up and watched it head down the next block.

"He must've seen that the storage door wasn't latched," I said as I hit the gas.

We careened around the corner in the opposite direction from the Mustang.

"Get the hell out of here!" Epstein hollered. "Those guys are going to kill me."

"Keep your britches on," I muttered.

I wasn't sure where the Mustang would go, but there were only so many ways out of the neighborhood. I reached the corner, turned right, and slowly approached the next intersection. I glanced up and down the street but didn't see the

Mustang. We weaved through the neighborhood, making my way back toward Colorado Boulevard. I was still a couple of blocks away when I saw the Mustang up ahead. I parked, flicked off the headlights, and waited.

"What are you doing?" Epstein asked.

"Sit still."

The Mustang turned the corner, and I pulled back into the street. When I reached the intersection, the Mustang had vanished. I drove down one more block, turned east, and reached Colorado Boulevard. I turned south, sped up, and got as far away from the junkyard as I could.

Epstein breathed a sigh of relief and leaned back against the seat. I kept glancing in the rearview mirror but didn't see the Mustang. I'd lost him.

We drove in silence for a few minutes. Epstein could've used a shower, and I think he knew that, because he rolled down the window a little to let in fresh air. When I stopped at a red light, I surveyed him. He had a bruise on the side of his face and a puffy lip. He swallowed hard and rubbed his eyes.

"You made someone really mad," I said. "What's going on?"

"I owe them money."

Epstein didn't try to bolt from the car. If he did, he'd be stranded. And he'd have to worry about McKane finding him. When the light turned green, I drove a little way ahead and turned into a strip mall parking lot.

"What are you doing?" Epstein asked.

I parked where I could see Colorado Boulevard, flicked off the headlights again, and turned to look at him.

"Tell me what's going on," I ordered.

Epstein gestured at the street. "Come on. What if he finds us?"

"Start talking, and then I'll get you home."

Epstein glared at me and threw up his hands. "I told you I owe them money."

I cocked an eyebrow at him.

"Okay, it's a lot of money. Over twenty grand."

I whistled. "How'd you get yourself into that kind of trouble? Do you drink? Gambling problems?"

He shook his head and started ticking things off on his fingers. "No. It's alimony and child support, and a mortgage, and car payments, and debt from our marriage. It all caught up with me. I got desperate, so I had to borrow the money, but my credit cards are maxed out."

"Then you started stealing."

"Well …"

"You're the neighborhood thief. You've been making money that way, right?"

"It's not all my doing. I think some of the street people in the neighborhood were already taking stuff. In fact, that's where I got the idea. I figured if everyone thought it was them or some druggies, no one would think to look at me."

"That was a pretty big risk," I said.

He shrugged.

"You took some jewelry from Shirley Durocher."

He hesitated. "Yeah. Someone left her windows open. I got inside and took a few things." He rubbed a hand over his face. "Please don't turn me in to the police. If I go to jail, I can't pay for my kids. I'll pay everyone back, I promise."

I thought about that. "I'll tell Holly and the others. It's their decision."

He didn't argue. "I'm starved. Can you go get me something to eat? I don't have any money, but I'll pay you back."

I stared at him. The obvious irony of this statement seemed to elude him. But he was also really hungry, and I pitied him.

"There's a Burger King down the street," I said. "How does that sound?"

"Anything."

I started the 4-Runner again and headed to the Burger King. I went through the drive-through, ordering us burgers, fries, and Cokes. When I got the food, I parked, gave him his food, and we started eating.

I thought about the electronic equipment I'd seen at McKane's apartment. "Let me guess. You were giving McKane some of the things you stole, right?"

He finished chewing a bite of burger, then said, "That's part of it, but I was supposed to give them a lot more cash by now. I didn't, so he came after me."

"That little squirt McKane doesn't look too formidable to me."

"He's not, so he sent his thugs after me. He's got a couple of cousins who you wouldn't want to mess with, trust me."

"How did you get involved with him in the first place?"

"It was a friend of a friend."

I cocked an eyebrow at him.

He held up a hand. "I know, it was shady from the start. But I was desperate, behind on my mortgage, and I didn't know what else to do."

"What all is McKane into?"

"Not just him, but his cousins. They fence stolen goods, they're loan sharks, they probably deal drugs, and who knows what else." He sipped some Coke, then shook his head. "I never should've listened to my friend. He told me to be careful, but I didn't realize what I was getting myself into. And now my friend knows I can't be trusted. What a mess I made for myself."

"If it makes you feel better, you have something on your friend as well."

"I don't know if he's doing anything illegal with them."

"Maybe, maybe not." I studied him for a moment. "You've surrounded yourself with some delightful people."

He snorted. "I told you, I was desperate."

"Let's get back to Shirley. You stole some jewelry from her. What else did you take?"

Even in the dark, I could see his face turning darker as he blushed. His eyes darted around, as if contemplating whether he should lie, but then he seemed to decide against it.

"That's all."

"A neighbor saw you leave her house the night she was murdered," I said.

"That wasn't me. I didn't go to her house that night. I stole the jewelry a few days after she died."

I stared at him. "Taking advantage of the situation, huh? You didn't like her, and you figured someone would think the murderer had taken the jewelry. Unless you're also the murderer."

He shrugged, but didn't say anything, just finished his burger.

"They said you yelled, 'You ornery old woman, you'll get what's coming to you.' "

Phil shook his head vehemently. "I never said anything like that. Alan Prestwick is the one who always calls her an ornery old woman."

"I heard you and Prestwick didn't get along. How do I know you're not just trying to point suspicion his way?"

"I'm not. He called her 'ornery.' "

I believed him. My mind raced as I thought about what Mr. Darmody had said to me. The night Shirley was murdered, he hadn't seen anyone, he'd only heard a male voice. Could he have mistaken Prestwick for Epstein? Even though Prestwick's wife had said he was home, what if she had been lying for him? I had my doubts about how truthful she'd been with me, and maybe that was it.

"I didn't murder Shirley Durocher," Epstein said. "Why don't you go talk to Alan? I think there was something going on between him and Shirley anyway. He'd been visiting her a lot lately."

"Was it about her complaints about you?"

"My accounting records are good."

"Why was she so suspicious of you?"

He looked away and gnawed his lip. "I did take some money," he finally said. "But I returned it. She overheard me talking on the phone to a friend about it, and she figured I was still stealing money."

"Were you?"

"No." His tone was firm. "My accounting records are perfect. You can ask Alan. I shared it all with him."

"When did you talk to Prestwick?"

"Tuesday."

That was the first day I'd been on the case. When I'd talked to Prestwick after that, he'd told me he hadn't talked to Epstein yet. It appeared he'd been lying to me, unless Epstein was lying to me now. Either way, I needed to talk to Prestwick again.

I started the 4-Runner and drove back to our neighborhood. Epstein and I didn't talk the entire way there. When I pulled up in front of his building, he turned and thanked me. He sounded sincerely grateful.

"I didn't have anything to do with Shirley's death," he said. "You can turn me into the police about the stealing, if you want. I made a big mistake, and it's time to make it right."

"Maybe there's a way to make this right without involving the police. It's going to cost you money to repay those you stole from, and maybe they won't turn you in. But if you don't straighten things out, I *will* report you to the police."

He nodded. "Thanks. I'll take care of things."

I gestured at his building. "Are you going to be able to get into your place?"

"The manager's usually around, and he'll have a key." He opened the door.

"Come over to my place if you can't get in."

He nodded again, got out, and hurried to his building entrance. Then he gave me a small wave before he disappeared inside. I waved back and drove away.

CHAPTER TWENTY-SIX

I pulled over at the corner and looked in the rearview mirror. I wanted to make sure that Epstein wasn't leaving again. I was pretty sure I believed him, but I wasn't taking any chances. While I watched, I called Alan Prestwick. His wife, Wanda, answered.

"Is Alan available?" I asked. "It's Reed Ferguson."

"I recognize your voice," she said. "Alan's not here. He's still at work."

I glanced at my watch. It was after eight.

"It's pretty late," I said.

"He's got a deadline on an important project."

"I'll try him at his office. If he comes home, would you be sure to have him call me?"

She hesitated. "I suppose I can do that."

Her voice was flat, almost depressed. I still had the feeling that she knew more than she was telling me.

I thanked her, gave Epstein's building one final look, then pulled into the street and drove to Seventeenth and Curtis. On the way, I called Willie to tell her I'd be out late. When she answered, I heard music and voices in the background. She sounded like she was having a good time, so I didn't keep her. I told her to tell Darcy hello, and then I ended the call.

When I got to Prestwick's building, I easily found a parking space on the street. I locked my car and walked to his building, but the front doors were locked and required a pass card. I doubted many people would be entering the building at this time of night, so I'd have no opportunity to slip in behind them. I would've preferred to surprise Prestwick in his office, but it looked like that wasn't going to happen. I'd have to call him, and see if he'd let me in.

I peered through the glass door, but didn't see anyone. I moved away from the door, pulled out my phone, and dialed Prestwick's office number. I got a recorded message and had to work my way through the directory until I found his extension. But when I dialed it, it rang and rang. I glanced back at the door, wondering if I'd missed Prestwick. I called his home, but his wife said he hadn't returned yet. She sounded slightly annoyed with me.

I was trying to figure out what I should do next when I saw Prestwick through the glass door. He had a briefcase in one hand and car keys in the other. He pushed through the glass door and started up the block in the opposite direction from me.

"Alan, may I have a moment of your time?"

He turned, then his eyes widened in surprise.

"What are you doing here?" he said, wrinkling his nose in exasperation and worry.

"I've been pursuing Shirley's murderer, and things have come back around to you."

"I have nothing to say to you."

He whirled around and trotted in the other direction. But when he reached the corner, he'd missed the light, and he had to wait for traffic to pass by. In the meantime, I caught up to him.

"You told me you hadn't talked to Phil Epstein about the accounting issues Shirley brought up," I said. "But Epstein said he talked to you on Tuesday, *before* I saw you."

Prestwick looked straight ahead, his lips a thin line under that heavy mustache. He didn't deny the lie, so I assumed I was right. I went on.

"You also said that you weren't at Shirley's the night she was murdered, but that's a lie too, isn't it?"

Now he turned to me. "I have nothing to say to you," he repeated.

The light turned green, and Prestwick marched across the street. I kept pace with him, but he wouldn't make eye contact with me. We passed a few people, but he was oblivious to them, his eyes straight ahead.

"Tell me I'm wrong," I said. "Phil Epstein said you frequently called Shirley an ornery old woman."

Now I got a glance, but he stayed silent.

"A neighbor heard someone call Shirley that very phrase the night she was murdered. Tell me it wasn't you. Give me something to work with."

I kept badgering him as he walked down the street.

"Epstein says that was your pet phrase for Shirley," I went on, "that she was an ornery old woman. Don't you think it's quite a coincidence that the neighbor heard someone call her an ornery old woman, and it wasn't you?"

Prestwick kept walking, and we reached the next corner. We had to wait for the light again. I kept at him. He finally turned and jabbed his fingers at me.

"Leave me alone," he snarled. "You have no idea what's going on."

"Tell me. I might be the only one who can save your neck, if you're innocent."

"How dare you think I murdered Shirley? I lov–" He gulped.

The light changed, but he just stood there staring at me. I thought about what he'd said about Shirley, how maybe people misunderstood her. And I wondered about the time Epstein said Prestwick had been spending with her. I ventured with a guess.

"You were having an affair with her, weren't you?"

Prestwick searched my face, and he finally nodded.

"Yes, I was having an affair with her."

"Care to tell me about it?"

It took him a minute, then he spoke. "It started a while back. I visited her a few times about some HOA matters, and at first it was innocent enough. She actually was a nice woman, she just didn't show that to the outside world." He ran a hand across his forehead, almost poking his eyes with his keys, but he didn't seem to notice. "Things with my wife haven't been going well. We managed to get through the stress of our bankruptcy and all our financial issues, but it took its toll on our marriage. We haven't been that close lately. And, I don't know, it was just nice to talk to Shirley." Now he fixed me with a hard gaze. "I would never have done anything to hurt her."

"What about calling her an ornery old woman?"

He shrugged and started walking again. "She could be ornery, what can I say? At times, she was so frustrating, I could've strangled her." He suddenly realized what he had said, and he waved a hand around as if to erase the words. "You know what I mean. I never hurt her."

"What about the night she was murdered? You visited her?"

We were part way down the block, and he turned into a parking lot.

"Yes. But I left a little after eleven."

That could've fit with what Mr. Darmody said, I thought.

"Your wife said you were at home," I said. "How could you be at home and at Shirley's house?"

He gnawed his lip as he walked up to a black Lexus. "Wanda thought I was home. She takes Valium at night to help her sleep. Once she does, she's dead to the world until morning. She wasn't lying when she said that I was at home. That's what she would think."

"That makes it easy for you to sneak out and cheat on her."

He glanced away, embarrassed. "I saw Shirley that night and came home. When I got there, Wanda was asleep, so she had no idea I'd gone out."

"Did anyone see you, either at Shirley's, or returning to your place?"

"No." He unlocked the car and threw his briefcase on the passenger seat, but instead of getting in, he closed and locked the door. "So you can't prove I killed Shirley."

"No, I can't prove or disprove it, because your alibi isn't solid."

"That doesn't mean I killed her." He ran his hand across his forehead again, then said, "I'm going to get a drink. It's been a long week, and I've been working a lot. I know I lied to you, that I didn't tell you I talked to Phil, but I'm telling you the truth about Shirley."

"Why lie to me about Phil? What was the point?"

"I was worried the police would find out I'd visited Shirley the night she died, and that they'd think *I* murdered her. I figured if I didn't tell you that I'd talked to Phil, and that his accounting books were good, maybe you'd look elsewhere for a while. And in the meantime, the real murderer would be found."

"That's pretty cold to let suspicion fall on Phil."

He stared at me. "I was upset about Shirley. I wasn't thinking clearly."

It was obvious he was hurting, but it was also a lame response.

"What about the conversation I overheard outside the HOA meeting? What was that *really* about?"

He bit his lip. "She threatened to tell my wife about the affair. I started to say I'd deal with her later when she slapped me."

That explained the noise I'd heard. "Deal with her how?"

"I wanted to talk to her, that's why I went over there later." He stepped away from the car. "I'm going to get a drink," he repeated. "Please leave me alone."

He hurried out of the parking lot and walked toward the Sixteenth Street Mall, two blocks away. I followed to the street corner, but went to my car, my mind on our conversation. Prestwick had no alibi, except for his wife, who I thought might be lying to me. I went over my conversation with her again. My gut said she was holding something back, and now I thought I knew what it was.

It was time to pay her another visit.

CHAPTER TWENTY-SEVEN

On the way to the Prestwicks' building, I pulled out my phone and called Wanda Prestwick again. Her voice sounded just as dejected as the last time I'd talked to her. Before she could say anything, I spoke.

"I need to talk to you again about the night Shirley Durocher was murdered."

"I don't—"

"Before you protest, you need to clarify a few things," I interrupted.

"What things?"

"Your husband was at Shirley's the night she was killed."

She sighed heavily, then said, "Not over the phone. Come on over. Alan's not here."

I thanked her and ended the call. Then a couple of things occurred to me. It wouldn't take me long to get to her place, but I hoped I hadn't given her the opportunity to run. And, I'd been wondering if she was lying about something. Had she known about the affair and murdered Shirley Durocher out of jealousy? Was I stepping into a trap now? I would have to be careful.

A few minutes later, I pulled into a parking place near the Prestwicks' building. I went into the little foyer, pressed the button for her condo, and waited. The door buzzed, and I went in and took the elevator upstairs. When I got out, I glanced up and down the hall. It was quiet. I made sure I could easily get to my Glock, then walked to the Prestwicks' apartment door and knocked. Wanda Prestwick opened the door, wearing a purple sweat suit and slippers.

"Come on in," she said, her voice still flat.

I stepped into the entryway and listened. It was quiet. I followed her into the living room. The TV was on, but the sound was muted, some talent show that I never watched. She gestured for me to sit on the couch, and she sank into the loveseat. She put her hands in her lap and stared at me, then seemed to think of her appearance and straightened her hair, even though it looked fine.

"What did you want?" she finally asked.

I glanced around, straining to hear anything, and was satisfied that we were alone.

As if she knew what I was wondering, she said, "Alan's not here, nor anyone else."

"Good. I think this is a conversation that needs to stay between you and me for now."

She gazed at me and blinked hard a few times. I was going to have to deliver some bad, and delicate, news to her. It was making me uncomfortable.

"I'm not really sure how to say this," I finally began, "so I'll just spit it out."

Before I could say another word, she said, "Alan was having an affair with Shirley, wasn't he?"

So much for catching her by surprise. I nodded. Her gaze

went to the TV, and she swallowed hard. Then she looked back at me, her eyes watery.

"I'm sorry," I murmured. "I just talked to Alan. He said that you were asleep when he went to see Shirley, but that he returned home around eleven."

"That was before Shirley was murdered."

I nodded. "You're his alibi, but he says you take Valium, and most nights you're dead to the world until dawn. That's how he would sneak out without getting caught." She didn't say anything, and I went on. "I saw the bottle of Valium in the kitchen, but I didn't know whose it was."

"The Valium's mine, that's true. But I didn't take any that night."

"That's why you knew about the affair."

She stared at the TV for a long time, and finally spoke. "I suspected it." She drew in a breath and let it out in a series of gasps. "I love Alan, but the bankruptcy was hard. We were distant, with lots going on."

That matched what Prestwick had said to me. I waited for her to continue.

"But I thought things were getting on the right track. Alan seemed a little bit better, more attentive. Then things seem to change again. The first thing I noticed was how he talked about Shirley Durocher. It was different than before. He was defending her behavior, where he hadn't before. Then it seemed like he had to visit with her more often, go over to her house to discuss things that had been brought up at the HOA meetings. That wasn't like him.

"I finally confronted him. I didn't outright ask if he was having an affair, but I said he'd suddenly seemed to be awfully chummy with Shirley. He denied it, of course, and said that she was an ornery old woman and how in the world did I think he'd be interested in her. After that, the meetings with her became less frequent. But then he started working late on a new project. I didn't think much about it at the time."

She shrugged her shoulders and shook her head, as if wondering about her own naiveté.

"Not too long ago, I had to call him at the office, and he didn't answer. And he wouldn't answer his cell phone, either. For some reason, that made me suspicious, when I hadn't been before. This was a few nights before Shirley was murdered. Then, the night she died, he had other excuses after the HOA meeting. I didn't protest, but I didn't take my Valium that night. Alan sneaked out, but I didn't let him know that I knew."

"It would've been easier if you'd told me this before."

She shrugged. "You came here, telling me that my husband might be a murderer. That was a lot to swallow, and I was having trouble processing it all." She held up her hands. "I didn't know what to do. I've been wondering about Alan ever since. I didn't know if I should tell him, or call the police, or what. Then you called." She stared at me, and her hands fell into her lap. "I figured I might as well tell you."

"So Alan was home at the time you say? This is the truth?"

"Yes." Her voice was as firm as I'd heard it all night. "I know you probably don't believe me, but it *is* the truth. Alan wouldn't have killed Shirley. I think ... I think he loved her, as hard as it is for me to say that."

I rubbed my chin for a second. "A lot of people kill the ones they love."

"Yes, but if you really know Alan, you'd know he didn't harm her. He was incredibly shocked by her death." A tear rolled down her cheek, and she wiped it away quickly. "I don't know where this leaves Alan and me, but I know he didn't kill Shirley."

I'd felt no threat from her, but there was a question I had to ask.

"Did you go see Shirley? Is Alan covering for you?"

She hung her head. "No, he's not. I suppose you don't know whether to believe that, either, but I've told you everything I know."

I contemplated her for a long time as she sat and stared at the floor. I concluded she was telling the truth. If so, where did that leave me? If Alan wasn't a murderer, then who was?

She finally looked up. "You said you'd seen Alan tonight. Where is he?"

"He was at the office, just as you said. But instead of coming home, he said he was going for a drink."

"He's been doing a lot of drinking since Shirley died."

"One more thing," I said. "Did Alan ever talk about Shirley's ex? A man named Bob Morrow?"

She shook her head. "Even when there wasn't anything going on between Alan and Shirley, he didn't say much about her, except that she frustrated him."

I had a hard time picturing Alan and Shirley together, but who was I to judge? Maybe there really was a softer side to her.

It didn't seem there was anything else to say, so I stood up. Wanda remained seated, wringing her hands in her lap.

"I appreciate your talking to me," I said. "I know I said this before, but if you think of anything else that might help me find Shirley's killer, I'd appreciate it."

She looked up at me. "I'll do that, but I really have told you everything."

I gave her a slight nod. She was still sitting in silence when I closed her door behind me.

CHAPTER TWENTY-EIGHT

I drove the short distance back to my building and parked. When I got out, I noticed a light on at Shirley Durocher's house. Maybe Holly was there, working. Then I thought about the note we'd found, the one someone had written about being tired of what Shirley was doing, and that "It ends now." If Bob Morrow hadn't written it, as he claimed, then who had? Now was as good a time as any to check on that.

I glanced around, wondering whether the murderer was around somewhere nearby, watching the house, or me. With that in mind, I was alert as I walked down the street toward her house. As I started up the walk, I kept an eye on the bushes in the darkness around the house. I didn't see anyone. I stepped up to the porch and knocked on the door, then waited. Holly opened it a moment later.

"Hi, Reed," she said. "Did you see the lights on?"

I nodded. "Do you have a few minutes?"

"Sure. You look disappointed. What's going on?"

She stepped back, and I entered the house. There were

some boxes in the hallway and in the living room. She'd been busy. Rock music played softly from the kitchen.

"Well ..." I said.

"Come on in." She gestured for me to follow her into the living room. "I've been trying to go through things. It seems like a never-ending task. I have leftover cupcakes. Would you like one?"

"Not now, but the one I had was fantastic."

"Thanks."

"Where is that note you showed me earlier?"

"It's here." She went over to the desk. "I found a few more notes from Bob, too."

"What did they say?"

"Here, you can read them." She took some papers from the desk and held them out.

I went over to her and took them. The handwriting was block letters, and the notes were cryptic, one apologizing that the money was late, and another saying 'here it is.' Another asked about Karen. I wondered if Shirley ever responded.

"The one you want to see is on the bottom," Holly said.

I flipped to the last one and studied it. This was the one that read, "We need to talk. I'm tired of what you're doing to me. It ends now." It was signed with a barely legible 'Bob', the first 'B' rather messy. I compared it to the other two notes.

"The handwriting is different."

She took the notes from me and looked back and forth between them. "You're right. I hadn't really noticed."

"And these two that you say are from Bob aren't signed. How do you know they're from him?"

"They were in an envelope with a return address of Dallas, Texas." She shrugged. "I figured they were from Bob."

I studied all the notes as I walked over to the couch and sat down. "Who is this signed note from, then, if not Bob?"

"I don't know." She knelt down beside a box and started putting some coffee table books into it.

"Do you need any help?" I asked.

She shook her head. "No, that's okay. What else have you found out?"

I set the notes down beside me. "I had an idea about who might've murdered your grandmother, but it's looking like a dead-end. I have an idea of what happened that night, or at least part of it. But I'm missing something."

She glanced up at me. "That's disappointing." She put her hands on the edge of the box and sighed. "It's crazy. I knew so little about my grandmother, but I feel like now, after she's gone, I'm really getting to know her through her things. Some of it, like the stuff with Bob, er, my grandfather, isn't so pleasant. She had a lot of interests, though, and I think she did some traveling that I never knew about."

"Have you been in touch with Bob?"

She bit her lip. "Not yet."

There was something in her tone. "What?" I asked.

She hesitated. "What did you think about him?"

I ran a hand through my hair. "It's hard to say. Honestly, he seemed like an okay guy, for someone who had just broken into your grandmother's house."

"But you don't think he killed Grandmother, do you?"

I shook my head. "No. I think he was just angry that she had been dishonest with him all these years, and that he paid her all that money."

"What else did your friend Cal say about him?"

"Just what he told you. Your grandfather lives in Texas, and he hasn't been in any kind of trouble." I made eye contact with her. "If you're not comfortable talking to him right now, wait until this is over. Then contact him, and see where it goes."

"I guess you're right." She stared at the box, but didn't move.

I picked up the notes again and compared them. "Did Shirley know another Bob?"

Holly shrugged. "I have no idea. It was a surprise finding out she'd been carrying on with Mr. Bonifacio." She let out a half-laugh. "I have a hard time picturing the two of them together."

"Me, too. Shirley didn't tell you anything about him?"

"No. She called him Bert, but I don't think anyone else did."

I leaned forward and stared at her. "What did you say?"

Her brow furrowed. "Just that Grandmother called Mr. Bonifacio 'Bert.' I think it was her nickname for him."

I grabbed the note that had been signed by Bob. I studied it closely, then handed it to her.

"What if that signature is 'Bert,' not 'Bob,' " I said. "Look, the second 'B' could be a 'T.' "

She looked at the note. "I suppose it could be."

"None of the notes from Bob were signed." I pointed at the one she held. "Why would he sign just that one?"

"I don't know."

I thought for a minute. Bonifacio had been sure to tell me that he'd seen someone else at Shirley's house when he'd left the night she was murdered. What if he was covering his own tracks? I'd missed something else as well. He'd also acted as if he'd never actually met Holly. Why had he lied about that?

I stood up. "I need to go."

Holly stared up at me. "Uh, okay." She held up the note. "You're going to talk to Mr. Bonifacio?"

"Yes. He hasn't been honest with me about some things." I held out my hand and gestured for the note. "May I take that?"

"Sure." She handed it to me. "Let me know what you find out."

"I will."

She was still staring at me as I headed out the door.

CHAPTER TWENTY-NINE

I hurried down the sidewalk, but when I headed for Mr. Bonifacio's, I stopped. Had I seen movement on the side of Shirley's house? I peered into the darkness, not sure whether I'd really seen something, or whether I was just tense and my mind was playing tricks on me. I crossed to the grass and up to the edge of Shirley's house. Then I paused and listened.

The side window to the house was open, and I heard the rock music faintly drifting through it. I strained to hear anything else.

Nothing but traffic sounds on the nearby streets.

I yanked out my phone and dialed the Embassy Suites Hotel. I asked for Bob Morrow's room and they connected me. It rang two times, and Morrow answered with a hesitant hello.

"You're there," I said.

"Who is this?"

"It's Reed Ferguson."

"You were expecting someone else?"

"No. For some reason, I thought you might be watching Shirley's house."

"Not a chance. I want to try to meet Holly and talk with her. At this point, I wouldn't do anything to jeopardize that."

"I think you're right about that."

"Will she talk to me?" He sounded both eager and sad.

"I think so. Just give her some time."

"Will do. Do you need anything else from me?"

"No."

I thanked him and ended the call. I peered into the night once more, and determined I must be crazy. The murderer wasn't watching Shirley's house. I went back to the sidewalk and hurried to Mr. Bonifacio's house. It was dark, with no lights on. I rang the bell and waited. After nothing happened, I knocked on the door, but no one answered.

"Where are you?" I murmured to myself.

I banged on the door a little harder with my fist, thinking maybe he was hard of hearing. When he still didn't answer, I tried the knob. Locked. I glanced around. The street was quiet, so I stepped off the porch and around the side of his house. I peeked in a living room window. The shades were almost closed, but I thought I saw someone sitting in a chair.

There was a chain-link fence and a gate near the back of the house. I studied the back yard. It was dark and quiet. I went through the gate and walked to the back porch. The rear door had a window, and I peeked into the kitchen. It was faintly lit by a light over the stove. I tapped on the door, but Mr. Bonifacio did not appear. I tried the knob and it turned. I looked around one final time, then let myself inside.

"Mr. Bonifacio?" I called out.

Nothing.

The kitchen smelled of garlic and tomatoes, as if he'd made spaghetti sauce, and my mouth watered. I listened and heard nothing. The kitchen was small, with only a small round table and two chairs in the corner. It was tidy and clean. I tiptoed into the living room. Someone was sitting in an overstuffed chair.

"Mr. Bonifacio?"

He didn't move. I crossed the room to an end table and turned on a lamp. The room suddenly lit up, and I turned around. Then I stopped short. Mr. Bonifacio was staring at me, but that's not what had turned my blood cold. It was the small gun in his hand. And it was pointed at me.

"What's going on?" I asked slowly.

He looked at me for a long time through his thick glasses. The gun never wavered.

"I wondered when you would come talk to me again," he finally said.

"Your first name is Roberto, but that's not what Shirley called you."

"That's right, she never called me that. She called me Bert." He snorted. "What a nickname."

"You were the one who left her the note, right?"

He squinted at me. "What note?"

"The one where you threatened her. 'It ends now.' Remember?"

"I didn't mean I was going to kill her. I just meant that it had to end."

"What did?"

He shrugged. "She shouldn't have been doing that to me. She knew what I thought about her. I loved her."

"What was she doing to you?"

"Alan."

My eyes narrowed. "For a while, I thought maybe Alan Prestwick had murdered Shirley. And that's what you wanted me to think. Did you actually see anyone that night, or were you making it up?"

He nodded. "I saw someone, and all I knew was that I didn't want you thinking I did anything."

"But Prestwick left earlier. You were just hoping to send me in a different direction."

I took a couple of steps toward him, and he held the gun a little straighter. I stopped and looked at him.

"What did you have against Alan?"

"I loved her, you know." His voice was soft.

Then it dawned on me. "Shirley was two-timing you, wasn't she? You were jealous of Alan and Shirley."

He didn't say anything to that.

"But why did you kill her?"

He lifted the gun. My hands stayed where he could see them. I had no idea what he was thinking, or what he might be capable of.

"I loved her," he repeated, "and instead of returning that love, she fooled around with Alan. Why would she do that to me?" His lip trembled.

"Tell me what happened that night," I said in a soft voice.

He glanced toward the window. Seconds ticked by before he answered. "I'd only recently found out that she'd been seeing Alan. I thought she and I had something special, but when I tried to talk to her about it, she would laugh at me."

"When Karen heard somebody arguing with her mother, it was you."

"Yes. I didn't understand why Shirley was doing that to me. She told me she'd stop, but I think she just said that to shut me up, because she kept seeing Alan. That night, I had a gut feeling that Alan would come over after the HOA meeting. He did a lot of times. I watched out my window, and sure enough, he showed up." His jaw tightened. "He was there for a while, and I knew what they were doing. I waited until he left, then went over to Shirley's house. At first, she didn't want to talk to me, but then she let me in. We talked for a while, and she just got nastier with me. She laughed at me and said I was a fool if I thought she loved me back. We were in the kitchen ... and ..." His voice choked. "We were arguing, and she kept telling me what a fool I was. I suddenly lost control, and I threw a glass vase at her. She ..." He put a hand to his mouth, then managed to say, "She fell to the floor and didn't move. I checked on her, but she was dead." He sniffled and rubbed his free hand over his eyes. "It was an accident. I never really meant to hit her. I was just so mad. Then I didn't know what to do, and I panicked."

"What about the broken glass?"

"I tried to clean it up, and then I left."

I stared at him for a moment. "You should've just told the police."

He drew in a ragged breath and let it out slowly. "It's easy to say that now. I didn't think anybody would believe me."

"Why don't we call the police now? I know the homicide detective who's investigating Shirley's murder. She's a good person, and she'll make sure you get treated fairly."

I started to reach into my pocket, and he aimed the gun higher.

"I don't want to go to jail. I'm an old man."

"Put the gun down and let's talk about this."

His hand began to shake, and then he lowered the gun. I dove toward him and knocked the gun out of his hand. It clattered across the room and lay there harmlessly. I'd almost fallen into Mr. Bonifacio's lap, and I righted myself and stepped back, ready for him to come at me. But what little fight he had was gone.

They say confession is good for the soul, and it apparently was for Mr. Bonifacio. He'd spent two days hiding the truth, but now the truth was out, and he was finished. He stayed motionless as I took out my phone and called 911.

CHAPTER THIRTY

Bonifacio and I waited in silence. It didn't take long for a squad car to show up. One uniform stayed with Bonifacio while the other took me out onto the porch and took my statement. Then he asked me to wait while he made a phone call. Then he made me wait longer, and finally Spillman's familiar blue Mustang drove up.

She had probably been at home when she got the call, because she was in jeans and a T-shirt with the logo for a local marathon. She came up the walk and gave me a look that I knew meant I was supposed to stay put. She went through the doorway and had a quiet conversation with the two uniforms, then joined me on the front porch.

"What's going on?" she asked.

I sighed. "I just told the uniform what happened."

"I want to hear it from you."

So I recounted everything. Spillman occasionally nodded and stopped me a few times to ask questions.

"That's it," I finally said.

She slowly raked a hand through her hair. "I wondered

about Bonifacio, but I couldn't find any proof." She glanced over her shoulder. "But you got a confession out of him. Good work."

"Thanks. May I go home now?"

She nodded. "Yeah, but don't leave town, okay? I'm sure we will have follow-up questions."

"No problem." I hesitated. "What about Holly?"

"I'll be talking to her soon."

"Tell her she can call me anytime."

"I will." She spun around abruptly and went back into the house.

With that, I was finally able to leave. On the way home, I called Cal, but he didn't answer. I left a message for him to call me as I started for the stairs on the side of my building. I heard voices, and the Goofball Brothers walked up from the back of the building.

"Hey, Reed," Ace said. "How's it going?"

"Just get back from playing pool?" I asked.

Deuce nodded. "Do you need any more help?"

I shook my head. "No, guys. The case is closed."

Ace stared at me. "What happened?"

I told them about Mr. Bonifacio, and they were both surprised.

"Wow, I would've never thought he was involved," Deuce said.

"Me, either," Ace agreed. "I feel bad for Holly."

His crush on her hadn't abated. I didn't dare tell him that I thought Holly might be interested in Cal. I thanked them for their help, and they disappeared into their condo, while I walked upstairs. The condo was quiet. Willie was sitting on the couch, holding Humphrey.

"Aren't you two cute," I said.

"Yes." She smiled at me. "I just got off the phone with your mother."

"Uh-oh."

"Don't worry, I talked her off the ceiling."

I sat down beside her. "Please tell me you didn't promise her grandchildren."

"No. But you are going to be forty soon."

"So there's plenty of time."

She laughed. "I'm not ready just yet either." Then she grew serious. "What's wrong?"

"I found Shirley's killer."

"Who?"

"Mr. Bonifacio."

"You're kidding."

"Nope." I told her the whole story. "I don't know what the police will do with Mr. Bonifacio. The whole thing is a shame."

"I feel bad for Holly."

"Me, too."

We sat in silence for a while, and I held her hand. She petted Humphrey, who seemed delighted with the attention. My mind was on Shirley. She may not have been a femme fatale, like Joan Crawford in *The Damned Don't Cry*, but the woman *did* get around. However, her dalliances shouldn't have caused her death.

"Let's go to bed," Willie finally said.

I took her hand and led her to the bedroom, and we forgot about the case. The next morning, I was cuddling with her when Cal called.

"What's up?" he said.

"I know who murdered Shirley Durocher." I told him about Mr. Bonifacio.

"Have you talked to Holly about it?" he asked.

"I'm going to call her this morning."

Willie nudged me. "Get Cal to meet us at the cupcake shop later today," she whispered. "We can all go to dinner, sort of a double date."

I rolled my eyes at her and received a glare. Then she poked me.

"I thought maybe we could go over there after work today," I said to Cal, "and maybe take Holly to dinner."

"Uh, I guess that would be okay."

"This will be a great way for you to ask her out, if you still want to."

He didn't say anything for so long, I thought maybe the call had disconnected. "Cal?"

"Okay. What time?"

"Five o'clock."

"See you there." He was gone.

"I hope he doesn't get so nervous that he doesn't show."

"If he really likes her, he'll show."

I sat up and stretched. "I guess I better get up. I've got to make sure that Holly will be available later today."

Willie grinned. "This'll be fun."

"Yes, you little matchmaker."

"Someone's got to help Cal along."

"Uh-huh. We'll meet him there at five."

"Great."

Willie looked delighted. I wondered what Cal would look like when we saw him later today.

I showered, then went into my office and called Holly.

"Detective Spillman talked to you?" I asked.

"Yes."

"How're you doing?"

She sighed. "Okay, I guess. In shock. I can't believe Mr. Bonifacio killed my grandmother."

"It's weird."

We talked about what Spillman had told her, and then I said, "There's more that I didn't tell the police."

"Oh?"

"It's about Phil Epstein." I told her about his burglaries, and his remorse. "How you handle it is up to you. But if he doesn't come clean to everyone he stole from, I'll call the police."

"Hmm, okay. I've got a lot to think about."

"True."

"Thanks, Reed. Send me a bill and I'll take care of it."

"How about I bring it by the shop, say around five? Then I can treat my wife to some cupcakes."

"That'd be great."

"Cal will be with us, too."

"Oh, okay. I'd ... like to see him." She sounded pleased.

"See you then."

I ended the call, satisfied I'd done my part to help Cal.

———

Promptly at five o'clock, Willie, Cal, and I walked into the cupcake shop. Holly was alone behind the counter. She greeted us warmly, and I introduced her to Willie. The two of them immediately started talking about cupcakes while Cal and I stood off to the side.

"You look good," I whispered to him.

He was neatly dressed in khakis and a striped shirt. He was so nervous, he barely spoke. Finally, Willie and Holly's conversation turned to Shirley when Willie offered her condolences.

"Thank you," Holly said. "I'm glad it's resolved. Reed, I can't thank you enough for helping me."

"No problem," I said. "Cal helped a lot, too."

She glanced at him shyly. "Thank you, too."

"You bet," Cal murmured.

We chatted for a few more minutes about her plans, and then Willie said, "We were just thinking we'd have dinner at Woody's."

Holly smiled. "I love their pizza."

Willie and I both signaled Cal with our eyes. Sweat broke out on his brow, and he cleared his throat, then looked at Holly.

"Holly," he said. "Would you like to join us?"

Holly smiled and nodded.

———

Turn the page *Double Iniquity,* Reed Ferguson mystery book 17!

"You're killing me!"

I stopped running and sucked in a tortured breath. My wife, Willie, glanced over her shoulder at me. Then she slowed down, turned, and jogged in place.

"Reed, you said you wanted to go for a run with me, so stop complaining."

"I can see I'm not going to get much sympathy from you," I said through gasps. I put a hand to my side and rubbed where an angry stitch was letting me know I hadn't been exercising enough lately. "I don't jog as much as you do."

Willie – real name Wilhelmina – was about twenty feet ahead of me. We'd jogged north and west from our condo in Uptown toward the City of Cuernavaca Park – only a couple of miles, but I was dying. She, on the other hand, was sailing along, looking sexy in running tights and a light gray insulated exercise jacket, with barely a drop of sweat on her pretty face.

"Come on." She spun around and ran off, then called out, "We need to hurry before it gets too dark."

It was just after five on an early December evening, and a

dusky gloom was settling in. Behind us, the lights of the buildings in downtown Denver winked on. Traffic whizzed by on Twentieth Street, oblivious to us.

Willie was far ahead as I started after her. What had I been thinking? I was not in shape and she was. *But*, I thought as I managed a hapless sigh, *it was good for me.*

Willie turned off Twentieth Street and into the City of Cuernavaca Park, a small green space by the Platte River that was popular with urbanites who lived nearby. When I reached the park, Willie was jogging onto the concrete path by the river. I followed her, and noticed the temperature drop near the water. I peered ahead, but Willie was nowhere in sight.

"Willie?" I yelled as I hurried down the path.

Then, in the shadows, I saw a figure in a gray jacket sprawled in the underbrush near the trail. Willie. I raced up to her.

"Are you okay?" I said as I bent down to check on her.

She nodded, and I helped her to her feet. Once I knew she was okay, I couldn't resist teasing her.

"What were you doing off the trail? Were you going to hide, then leap out and scare me when I went by?"

She shook her head. "I thought I heard someone yelling, maybe for help." She gestured toward a bridge that spanned the river. The water gurgled below us, and the hum of traffic was all around. "Maybe I was mistaken. Regardless, as I stepped off the path, I tripped."

I put my hands on my hips. "Are you kidding? At this time of night, you shouldn't be wandering off the trail. You don't know who might be lurking around the bridge, or anywhere else around here."

She held up a hand. "I know, I'm always careful. But I thought I heard someone."

"Then call for help, or wait for me," I chided her. I looked around and strained to hear over the sounds of the river. "Is someone there?"

She shrugged. "I don't know. But there's that." She pointed at the ground, where a small black duffel bag sat near the underbrush.

"Who does that belong to?" I asked.

"Search me."

I grinned. "Tempting."

We both contemplated the bag for a moment, then turned toward the river.

"Hello?" I called into the dusk. "Anyone around?"

A lone jogger passed by on the trail, her ponytail bobbing as she ran.

"Did you see anyone near the trail?" Willie called out to her. The woman shook her head, but didn't stop. Willie frowned. "That wasn't very helpful."

"I doubt she was nearby when you tripped," I said.

I took a few steps toward the bag, then bent down. It had a white zipper and an Adidas logo.

"Be careful." It was her turn to chide me. "What if there's a bomb in there?"

"Unlikely."

I prodded the bag, then noticed the zipper was undone, so I opened it. We both looked inside.

"It's paper," Willie murmured.

"Money." I stared into the bag. "Lots of it." I glanced up and down the river bank. "Do you see anyone?"

She shook her head. "Just us."

I stuck a hand in and rifled around.

"Don't you dare pretend like something bit your hand to scare me," Willie warned me.

I glanced at her. "Or what?"

"Reed."

I chuckled as I continued to search the bag.

"There's nothing in here but stacks of bills," I announced. "Lots of twenties, and some fifties and hundreds." I tried to count it, but lost track. It was a lot.

"Drug money?"

"That's a good guess."

Willie whistled. "What do we do with it?"

I sat back on my haunches. "I can't find a label or anything to tell us who this belongs to."

I stood up and moved toward the river and looked around.

"Where are you going?" she asked. "If you don't want me wandering around in the dark, you shouldn't either."

I took a few more steps and stopped. "Fair enough." I peered into the gloom. "Are you sure you heard someone?"

She shook her head. "Not positive."

I returned to the bag and picked it up.

"What are you going to do?" she asked.

I waved a hand around. "We can't just leave it here."

"Just because you're a detective, doesn't mean you need to investigate this situation."

"A private investigator," I said, sounding a lot like Tom Selleck's character Magnum. He hated being called a detective. I really wished I sounded more like my hero, Humphrey Bogart. He made everything look cool, and I aspired to be a cool private investigator like Sam Spade, who Bogie played perfectly.

"You sound miffed, like your mother sometimes does."

My jaw dropped. "Oh, that's cold."

I love my mother, but she does miffed better than anyone I know. They say you become your parents, but good Lord, was I turning into my *mother*? The horror ...

Willie smiled, then grew serious. "Shouldn't we call the police?"

I frowned. "We could, but I'm sure they'd tell us to wait for them."

"For how long?"

"Hm. Hard to say. This isn't an emergency, so they're not going to race here with lights blazing. And if they're tied up with other calls, it could be quite a while before they get here."

We contemplated the bag for a moment. Then she rubbed her arms and shivered.

"This can't be anything good. Do you think the person who left it here – or maybe whoever's supposed to pick it up – is watching us right now?"

I did a one-eighty, staring into the darkness. *Was* someone out there? Would that person try to harm us in order to get the bag back?

"I don't feel safe here, Reed," she whispered.

I nodded. I thought for just a second longer. "Yeah, me neither. But I also don't feel okay just leaving the bag behind. It's getting cold. Let's get out of here. We'll take it home, and I'll call Spillman."

Detective Sarah Spillman is a homicide detective with the Denver Police Department. Over the course of many of my investigations, our paths had crossed, and she and I had become friends. Although it may have been unorthodox to turn over the money to a homicide detective, I preferred that over a random call to the department. I was sure there would be a lot of questions about us finding the bag, and having the department know I was friends with Spillman seemed a good thing.

I pointed toward the riverbank. "If for some reason the police want to know where we found the money, I'll come back here and show them."

"That sounds like a good plan." Willie shivered again. "Better than you getting involved in this."

"In what?" I laughed. "We're just turning over this bag to the police. No big deal."

"I'll bet they'll have questions."

I nodded. "It's no big deal," I repeated.

How many times had I thought that before? And how many times had I been wrong?

Too many to count.

———

Keep reading _Double Iniquity_, Reed Ferguson Mysteries, book 17: reneepawlish.com/DbIwb

FREE BOOK

Sign up for my newsletter and receive book 1 in the Reed Ferguson mystery series, *This Doesn't Happen in the Movies*, as a welcome gift. You'll also receive another bonus!

Click here to get started:
reneepawlish.com/RFDW

RENÉE'S BOOKSHELF

Reed Ferguson Mysteries:
This Doesn't Happen In The Movies
Reel Estate Rip-Off
The Maltese Felon
Farewell, My Deuce
Out Of The Past
Torch Scene
The Lady Who Sang High
Sweet Smell Of Sucrets
The Third Fan
Back Story
Night of the Hunted
The Postman Always Brings Dice
Road Blocked
Small Town Focus
Nightmare Sally
The Damned Don't Die
Double Iniquity
The Lady Rambles

A Killing

Reed Ferguson Novellas:
Ace in the Hole
Walk Softly, Danger

Reed Ferguson Short Stories:
Elvis And The Sports Card Cheat
A Gun For Hire
Cool Alibi
The Big Steal
The Wrong Woman

Dewey Webb Historical Mystery Series:
Web of Deceit
Murder In Fashion
Secrets and Lies
Honor Among Thieves
Trouble Finds Her
Mob Rule
Murder At Eight

Dewey Webb Short Stories:
Second Chance
Double Cross

Standalone Psychological Suspense:
What's Yours Is Mine
The Girl in the Window

The Sarah Spillman Mysteries:
Deadly Connections
Deadly Invasion

Coming Fall 2020

The Sarah Spillman Mystery Short Stories:
Seven for Suicide
Saturday Night Special
Dance of the Macabre

Supernatural Mystery:
Nephilim Genesis of Evil

Short Stories:
Take Five Collection
Codename Richard: A Ghost Story
The Taste of Blood: A Vampire Story

Nonfiction:
The Sallie House: Exposing the Beast Within

CHILDREN'S BOOKS
Middle-grade Historical Fiction:
This War We're In

The Noah Winter Adventure Series:
The Emerald Quest
Dive into Danger
Terror On Lake Huron

ABOUT THE AUTHOR

Renée Pawlish is the author of The Reed Ferguson mystery series, *Nephilim Genesis of Evil*, The Noah Winter adventure series for young adults, *Take Five*, a short story collection that includes a Reed Ferguson mystery, and The *Sallie House: Exposing the Beast Within*, about a haunted house investigation in Kansas.

Renée loves to travel and has visited numerous countries around the world. She has also spent many summer days at her parents' cabin in the hills outside of Boulder, Colorado, which was the inspiration for the setting of Taylor Crossing in her novel *Nephilim*.

Visit Renée at www.reneepawlish.com.

 facebook.com/reneepawlish.author
twitter.com/ReneePawlish
 instagram.com/reneepawlish_author

CPSIA information can be obtained
at www.ICGtesting.com
Printed in the USA
LVHW032335070321
680815LV00005B/1078